TWISTED

TAINTED TALES

JANINE PIPE

Published by Pipe Screams Press

Copyright 2021 Janine Pipe

Interior formatting by Jason Brant

Edited by Ben Long

Cover Illustration Neil Fraser, Neil Fraser Graphics www.neilfrasergraphics.com

All rights reserved. No portion of this book may be reproduced, stored in any retrieval system, or transmitted at any time or by any means mechanical, electronic, photocopying, recording or otherwise without the prior, written permission of the publisher.

The right of Janine Pipe to be identified as the author of this work has been asserted by her in accordance with the Copyright, Designs and Patents act 1988.

First published 2021

This is a work of fiction. Names, characters, businesses, places, events and incidents are either products of the author's imagination or used in a fictional setting. Any resemblance to actual persons, living or dead, or actual events is purely coincidental.

The following selections, some in different form, were published previously:

"Footsteps" in *Diabolica Britannica* edited by Keith Antony Baird in 2020

"Sweet Child O Mine" On Ghost Stories the podcast 2020

"Tainted Love" on Tales to Terrify 2020

"It's a Sin" On Ghost Stories – the podcast 2020

"They" in *Alien Agenda Sampler 2020*, edited by Glenn Rolfe in 2020

CONTENTS

Foreword   vii
Introduction   ix

Track One   1
Track Two   22
Track Three   30
Track Four   40
Track Five   48
Track Six   57
Track Seven   63
Track Eight   72
Track Nine   78
Track Ten   94
Track Eleven   101
Track Twelve   115
Track Thirteen   124
Track Fourteen   135
Track Fifteen   143
Track Sixteen   153
Track Seventeen   161

Trigger Warnings   175
Spotify Playlist   177
Acknowledgments   179
Acknowledgements and Praise   183
About the Author   185

PRAISE FOR TWISTED

Are you ready for cinematic vibrancy in your stabby horror fiction? Memorable, foul-mouthed, kick-ass characters? Janine Pipe is on the scene, loud as a whip-crack with roller-coaster-style fun.

Sadie Hartmann – Mother Horror

Like Grady Hendrix's demented little sister, Janine Pipe takes us on a splattery pop culture joyride in a bitchin' Camaro on fire with a congealing pile of human viscera in the back seat. Hang on for the ride, and don't ask any questions. Just go with it. You'll have such a gory good time with her.

Kenzie Jennings, author of *Reception* and *Red Station*

A mixtape of pure terror! This collection is dripping with nostalgia, extreme violence and buckets of bodily fluids. A strong debut!

Joshua Marsella, author of *Scratches* and *Severed*

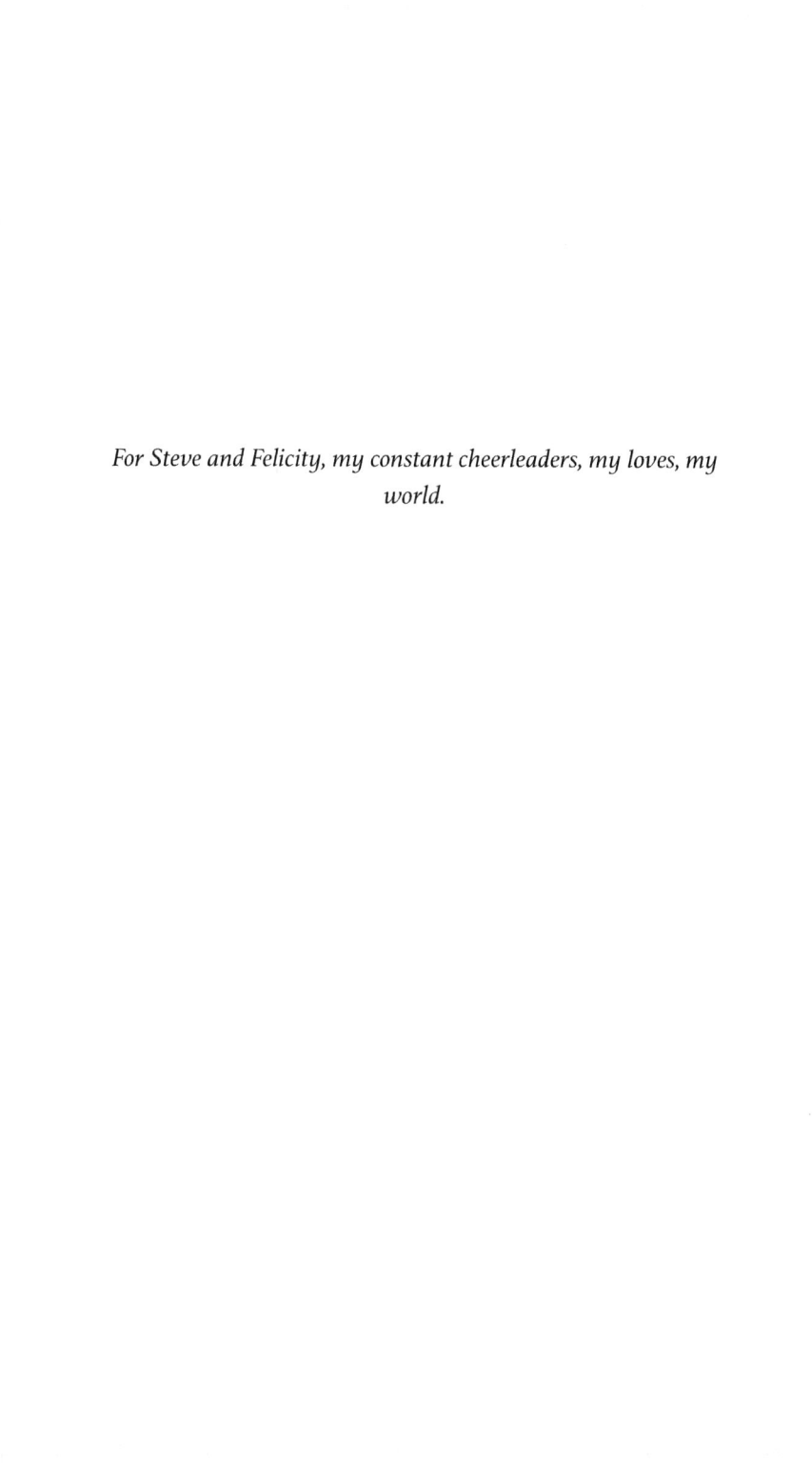

For Steve and Felicity, my constant cheerleaders, my loves, my world.

FOREWORD

The 2020 pandemic was a huge, scary piece of shit. It was something that crawled up from the bowels of our sewers and attempted to fuck us like Brett (aka the "smart motherfucker") tried to fuck Marsellus Wallace in *Pulp Fiction*. But you know what? Just like Jules and Vincent standing in that room, some of us got served something miraculous.

I managed to put out a book. And with that book, not only did I make a new fan, I made a friend. She's kind and cool. She's super supportive of our horror community, and our kiddos even became pen pals!

Yeah, Covid has been pretty fucking bad, but for us writers, especially the ones that got sent home from work for a bit, we had more time to read, more time to talk, and more time to discover new voices.

Well, wasn't I surprised when this new fan, this new friend turned out to be a writer. Okay, I wasn't *that* surprised. I published one of her stories in a sampler for my publishing company ("They"–which can be found in this very collection). I thought the story showed great potential and proved that she not only loved and cared for our community, but she was destined to glide from reader/reviewer to author. And when she reached out to me to ask if I'd write a foreword to her first collection, I did not hesitate to say yes.

Now dig this, I knew Janine was awesome. I knew she was a good writer with a future in this business. When I sat down to write this up, I figured I'd read a handful of the stories she sent me and scribble a nice piece. Well, I started reading... and I couldn't stop. The few stories turned into the whole book!

She doesn't just have *potential*, Janine has the gift.

"Footsteps" is a fantastic opener. A declaration of sorts. No wonder it was nominated for a Splatterpunk Award! While Janine shows an ease and flare with her splattery set of tales, when I read "When Doves Cry", I said "Holy shit! That was amazing!" As writers, most of us don't want to be pigeonholed. We don't want to be locked in a box. The best authors are able to switch things up from story to story or book to book. After reading "Footsteps" and then "When Doves Cry," the idea of reading just a few stories was no longer in the realm of possibilities. This woman is more than *just a fan*, she's fucking got it, man. And I'm glad to count her not just as a friend, but also as a peer.

So get on board, motherfuckers, and let the miracles happen. Take a break from this messy real world and escape with a collection of stories that will take you away, bring you back to your youth, rip your fucking face off, get you hot and bothered, and infect you with the need to collect fingers or devour someone in the woods beneath a full moon. Let it be known– Janine Pipe has arrived.

-Glenn Rolfe
March, 2021

INTRODUCTION

Hello. My name is Jill, and I am a junior solicitor at Jeffery, Yardley and Marshall. Sometimes I get to perform extremely interesting duties like litigation, and other times I get dumped with the mundane tasks no one else wants to touch. Thus, when Mr Jeffery asked me to attend an empty property we had been lumbered with, to see if there was anything of value left before the clearance people attended, I couldn't have been more thrilled. Did you sense the sarcasm?

I didn't know much about the case. The police had been involved since it belonged to some semi-famous writer who'd gone missing. Like one of her stories, she'd just upped and vanished without a trace. They had already removed any potential evidence – bank statements, laptops, diaries etc. I wasn't exactly sure what I was even meant to be looking for.

She'd either been a meticulously tidy and organised person, or the police had been thorough as there wasn't too much left to go through. Being a bit of a bookworm myself, I was most interested to investigate her study-cum-library. There was a beautiful old desk in the middle of the room. Of course, the computer had been taken away, but upon closer inspection I found a wad of papers in one of the drawers. The police hadn't presumed them prevalent to any criminal or suspicious activity, but I soon realised I was holding a plethora of her unpublished short stories.

Oh, and a mixtape. You know, a cassette, something people used before CDs and digital downloads.

Over the coming pages, I shall share with you my findings...

These stories won't be for everyone. At the back of the book, you will find a list of potential trigger and content warnings. Please consult them before each story if you have any concerns. Thank you.

TRACK ONE

*J*ill - *I wasn't exactly sure what I had been expecting to find as I dug through the piles of old papers that had been locked inside the desk drawer. Since it was all being dumped anyway, I had just broken in. I've never been able to resist a mystery. I didn't see anything amiss with taking them home to look at. Of course, I knew the owner had been a writer and had kept her latter work hidden away. Wrinkling my nose and sneezing as the layer of dust revelled in its newfound freedom, I peered closely at the handwritten notes in front of me. I marvelled at the cursive lettering, penned in ink upon the now yellowing pages. It appeared I had happened upon her true passion, unbeknownst to me, she had been a keen creator of the macabre.*

Over the following pages, you will find some of the tales I discovered in those dusty drawers, paper so fragile it would have fallen to pieces had it not been handled with care.

The first of which I present to you now.

It seems she enjoyed taking risks, testing boundaries. The world of extreme horror had been long dominated by men, with many wrongly presuming women couldn't and wouldn't be able to match their male counterparts when it came to gratuitous sex, violence, gore and excessive bodily fluids. See what you think. I regard it as a cautionary tale. About friendship and camping. Women and relationships. And blood. So much blood.

Be careful next time you go into the woods. And always be sure to *plug it up*.

Number 1 - Footsteps

Come on, just a few more minutes.

Kelly was desperate. She tried to convince herself her bladder was not about to explode all over her new Ford Escort.

Please, please, please.

She hadn't planned to leave quite so late and had in no way intended to take the winding, no-cats-eyes route through the forest.

It was about fifteen minutes at least until she would arrive home.

Duran Duran's latest hit blasted out from the radio.

Lady Luck was not on her side. She felt a sharp pain and realised with annoyance that not only did she need to pee, but her sanitary pad was now sodden too.

She pulled the car over.

God damn it!

She sat for a moment considering her options. She in no way wanted to do what she was now considering. She was not uncouth.

Yet, if she didn't get out and change her now useless pad, she risked leaking menstrual blood all over the cream interior of the new car.

Needs must.

She grabbed her bag and a bottle of water and turned the headlights on to full beam. It was pitch black in the woods and she hadn't seen another car for miles. With the added light of her open driver's door, she would be able to pee, change her pad, bag it up, rinse the ground and her hands and be on her way. Desperate times, desperate measures. She would never speak of it.

She stepped out onto the grass verge, pulled up her dress and squatted.

Relief was short-lived.

Crack.

She froze, knickers around her ankles, pad in hand.

What the—

Kelly didn't even get the chance to scream.

'HAVE you got all the cameras, the batteries, the extra batteries? Everything is charged and ready to go?'

'Yes,' Felicity replied, feeling exasperated. They had already gone over this several times.

'Tent, maps, torches, food? I really don't want to get stuck out in the woods tonight without adequate provisions.'

'It is all sorted,' she promised, rolling her eyes.

'And we know where Loz is waiting for us?'

'Yes, Becky! Loz is *exactly* where she said she would be, like we have discussed. Chill!'

She was looking forward to their overnight adventure in the woods. It seemed a bit cliché, rite-of-passage, but the girls thought it would be good for their book research.

Becky, however, was getting a little fanatical about what

they were taking with them. She was not an outdoorsy type of person and was paranoid that they would forget some 'can't spend the night without' essential.

She was dressed as if she was off to a party rather than hiking through the forest. Low-rise jeans with a floral peasant top might be perfect for a night at the Student Union, but not so great for traipsing through the woods. At least Felicity had managed to convince her she needed hiking boots, to protect her from twisting an ankle.

Growing up with three older rough-and-tumble brothers, Felicity had spent many days climbing trees; and many evenings camping as a Brownie. She had chosen sensible cargo trousers and a ribbed turtleneck sweater. Her long blonde hair was tied into a ponytail under a Von Dutch baseball cap.

She did feel some trepidation. Only insofar that whilst researching several of the so-called local legends of the area, she had discovered there were many tales regarding unexplained disappearances. But she was a sceptic. Despite thoroughly enjoying digging through the old lore, she didn't think anyone could just vanish. Truth be told, she was hoping in the main to get some good photos. One might prove worthwhile for the cover of her book, if it were to ever be published of course.

Sighing deeply, she listened as Becky continued to fret about whether they had packed enough food for the one-night sleepover and making sure they didn't have anything that would attract 'wild animals'.

Felicity snorted. 'I'm pretty sure there aren't any bears or wolves in Dorset. Maybe a nosey pony?' She checked the bags and camping apparatus were secure under the trailer tarpaulin and got into the Range Rover she was borrowing from her dad for the trip.

'Just get in!' she ordered, and as always, Becky dutifully obeyed her. Sometimes it was more like having a puppy than a best friend.

'You certain you know where we're going?' Becky asked as Felicity put the 4x4 into gear and tore off the pebbled driveway.

'Yes, it's not far. And it's a *huge* forest. How damn hard can it be to find? Besides,' she added, 'Loz is already there, remember.'

Becky furrowed her brow. She often seemed stressed these days. She fidgeted for a bit and then played with the radio, settling on some classic 80s rock.

Felicity turned and looked at her friend. 'Try not to think about him, Bex. This is for us. Fuck him.'

Becky blinked a few times, as if fighting back tears. Then she rummaged in her bag and pulled out a packet of cigarettes. Her ex had never liked her to smoke.

She put one in her mouth, lit it, and took a long drag.

'Yeah!' she shouted. '*Fuck him*! Oh, that reminds me.' She turned, sighing. 'Typically, I got my period today. I can't believe the timing of it! Because being all bloody in the woods is so convenient. Not.'

Felicity concentrated on driving. It was typical that Becky would have to suffer some sort of minor setback on the trip. This was less than ideal, but not the end of the world. She understood what was implied. At least that bastard hadn't left her pregnant.

They drove on in companionable silence. It took around half an hour to find the start of the woods. It seemed to go on for miles and miles. And as was to be expected, the GPS and mobile phone coverage was now intermittent.

'So', she said, glancing over at Becky, who was holding the map, frowning. 'Where exactly is Loz?'

Becky turned the map upside down, and then gave an exasperated sigh. 'I just don't know!' she whined. 'You're the expert – *you* find her.'

So, Felicity continued to drive down the windy dirt path, until they came to an area that seemed as though it had been used by campers before. And there, thank goodness, was Loz's battered Mini. She parked the car and hopped out, enjoying a luxurious stretch as she did.

'This should be it.' She could see a well-trodden path in front of them, and the trees appeared to be a little sparser in the distance. They didn't want to traipse too far in. Hopefully they'd soon spot Loz who had texted earlier that morning to say she was on the way, but her Nokia 8110 was about to die. Typical of her.

They hauled off the tarp and pulled the heavy packs onto their backs. They grabbed the tent and the foodstuff, and Felicity made sure the Range Rover was secure.

Then off they went into the woods.

THEY WALKED for about ten minutes or so until they came upon base camp. The floor was clear of rocks and debris, and there was plenty of shelter, should the weather take a turn for the worse. Loz's bright pink tent was set up, complete with a small pit for a fire later. Although, strangely, there was no sign of *her*.

They set down their belongings and started on the tent.

When they were done, Becky flopped onto an old rug and pulled a bottle of Jack Daniels from her bag.

'Cheers, dahling', she quipped, before taking a huge gulp of the liquor. She lit another cigarette and got out a notepad.

'So, according to The Plan, once we are set up, we take some photos of 'trees' and see if we can witness anything 'spoooooky'.'

Becky exaggerated the last word and giggled at herself.

'Well okay then.' Felicity grabbed her camera and rolled her eyes at her friend. She hoped she wasn't just going to get pissed and ruin the research. She might not believe in any of the stupid legends, but if she was going to write a book, then she needed to at least *see* some of the locations where the so-called disappearances had taken place.

'I hope the woods don't get all *Blair Witch* on us,' she chuckled, making sure the camera was charged and she had spare batteries. 'And where the hell is Loz?'

Becky hiccupped and announced, 'Let's go find her!'

Felicity shook her head, but agreed it was the best plan. She had tried calling her on the off chance there might be a signal, but inevitably it had gone straight to voicemail. Loz had said the phone was almost dead. As your stereotypical hippy-artist type, she shouldn't be too hard to find. They'd just follow the smell of patchouli and hope for rainbow tie-dye in the distance.

Further into the forest, they headed.

BECKY STUMBLED on a rock and swore. She crouched down rubbing her shin, then took a swig from her hip flask, much to Felicity's frustration.

Sighing, she reached for the camera and pointed at various aspects of the trees and trickling water. Suddenly Felicity noticed that aside from the stream, it was quiet, eerie. Anyone with an overactive imagination could rustle up a story involving Dorset's very own Bermuda Triangle.

You would expect to hear the wind in the trees at the very least. Shouldn't there be a cacophony of bird noises?

'Hey, Bex? Don't you think it's kind of quiet, like too quiet out here?' she asked.

Becky yawned and peered over at her. 'Nope,' she replied, 'I like it. It's,' she frowned, as if struggling to find the right word, 'um, peaceful.'

But something was off. Becky obviously wasn't picking up on it. Felicity was annoyed with her. Sure, she had always been a bit of a party girl, she liked to drink, smoke, slept with the wrong guys. But did she need to get sozzled right now, when they were trying to get some work done?

And where the fuck was Loz? It was just like her to bugger off and do her own thing, then appear at the end of the day as if nothing had happened. She did it all the time. But surely, she wouldn't have wandered off too far without them?

Continuing to take pictures, she paused to check her work so far on the digital screen. Honed in on a creepy, gnarled old tree towards the end of her natural sightline, and now, scrutinizing the image, there appeared to be something else in the shot.

What the—? she thought and zoomed in on the screen. It was now a tad blurry, but it appeared that there was something peeking out from behind the tree. She peered in the direction again and fired off several shots with the camera, then viewed them on the display. It was gone. Whatever it was, a trick of the light perhaps, it only showed up on one picture. She shook her head as if trying to make sense of it. Sure, there were all sorts of animals out there, but this, it seemed well, tall?

I'm losing the plot, she thought, *all this shite about spooky tales is messing with my head*. She walked over to Becky and picked up the flask. She took a huge gulp of the firewater, gasping as it burned her throat.

She decided not to tell Becky about the photo, yet. Not feeling remotely comfortable in this spot, Felicity suggested they head back to camp for some food and to see if there was any sign of Loz.

'Great!' agreed Becky immediately, 'I need to piss and change this tampon. God, I hope none of the animals out here can smell me? Don't they get attracted to period blood, is it like a turn on for them?'

'Ew!' she laughed, 'what sort of sick shit have you been reading? I've told you to stay off the internet! Also, I don't think any type of animal is going to want to fuck you just 'cause you're on your monthly!'

Grinning, Becky replied, 'What, am I not hot enough for some rabid dog to come looking for some action?'

They laughed at the absurdity of the suggestion, and some of the tension she had felt began to ease away; perhaps aided by the very generous intake of Jack Daniels.

They managed to find their way back to the camp, where they made a small fire and heated up some tins of sausages and beans. They devoured the food then rinsed out the pots so as to try not to attract any 'visitors'.

She decided to show Becky the photo. 'What do you think it is?' Felicity asked cautiously. 'Trick of the light, just a normal forest animal being nosey or some kind of fucked-up wolf-man?' She had meant the last part to come out as flippant, but as she said it, something felt tight in the pit of her stomach. Fear?

Becky squinted at the camera screen. She screwed up her eyes and put it up close to her face.

'Huh,' she said.

'Huh? All you can say is huh?'

'Well,' Becky began, 'it sort of looks like, a fucked-up wolf-man.'

The ice cold feeling inside of her began to grow. She had expected, prayed, that her best mate would pooh-pooh the idea.

'Come on,' she said. 'This is England, not the Pacific coast of America! We don't have wolves or bears. It must be—'

'Let's go back and find the tree,' cried Becky, cutting her off mid-sentence. 'We can see if there is like fur and footprints or shit. Or,' she said giggling, 'like ripped up bunny bodies hanging from branches, ha ha.'

Clearly the bourbon was stronger than she had thought.

Get a grip, Felicity told herself. *You wanted photos and 'evidence' for your project, you now have a perfect chance to get something.*

'Okay,' she said, sounding braver than she felt. 'Let's grab some supplies and head out. There's a couple of hours before it starts to get dark, and we should stay at the camp then. Loz will hopefully wander back once her belly rumbles,' she added.

Becky grabbed the backpack with their wallets and keys, and refilled the flask, then lit another cigarette and declared she was ready. She rubbed her belly, and took a handful of painkillers, washed down with Mr Daniels.

They headed out of the camp and back toward the river. They walked a little further upstream this time, in the direction of the old tree. As they got closer to the clearing, Felicity grew trepidatious. She got out her camera and started to take photos of the scenery. Perhaps that would somehow calm her. Seeing the world from behind the lens made it seem almost dreamlike.

'Shit!'

She spun around to face Becky, who was just a few feet away.

'What the fuck is *that*?'

They had reached the tree.

She froze.

Felt her chest tighten and bile rise in her throat.

'I'm gonna...' Becky began, and then bent over and vomited.

They had only been able to see the front of the scene from their previous vantage point. Now she witnessed something she knew she would never, ever be able to forget. There were huge mounds of dirt and leaves all over the ground, streaked red with blood. There seemed to be pieces of flesh and bones sticking out of each of them, as if they were some sort of sick and twisted pantry. But that wasn't even the worst of it. Strung from the branches behind the huge, gnarled old tree were the skins and pelts of what she hoped and prayed were animals. Huge animals. Deer, maybe a pony? What the fuck was crazy enough to attack a bloody pony?

There was something else too. Something small, silver and shiny. Hanging in the branches high above their heads. More than one.

'Are they—' she began when Becky interrupted.

'I don't feel so good,' she started, when suddenly, they heard a noise.

Snap.

'Run,' Felicity hissed. She didn't know, didn't care what had made that sound, but she realised it was the very first thing that they had heard other than themselves since they got there, and there was no fucking way she was going to wait around to find out what it was.

She wanted to race back to camp, grab their stuff and

motor out of there as fast as she could. They needed to find Loz and leave immediately.

Becky, however, didn't seem to be sensing the urgency. She had dropped to her knees, the backpack with the supplies discarded next to her.

Felicity seized the bag and put it on her own shoulder. She grabbed Becky's arm, 'Come on, Bex, we need to move *now*!'

Somehow, she managed to convince Becky that they needed to get up and make a run for it. She held her arm as she guided them back through the trees. In her blind panic, she couldn't be one hundred percent sure of the way that they had originally travelled. Now, it all seemed the same and she could feel the anxiety and dread building in her chest. Becky was sobbing now, which wasn't making things any easier. She needed to concentrate.

'This way,' she said, thinking, *hoping*, she had recognised the path into a clearing that would lead back to the campsite.

Crack.

Something was now extremely close behind them. It was almost too much to bear. Becky let out a banshee-esque screech at the top of her lungs, and in her desperation to flee, managed to knock Felicity to the ground. As she landed in an awkward fashion, she twisted her ankle. Spiky foliage lacerated her hands with their tiny daggers as she broke the fall. Crying out in pain she glanced up...but Becky was gone.

'No!' she yelled, 'Bex!'

BECKY HAD MADE off in complete and utter booze-and-terror-filled panic. She didn't know where she was headed or where she would end up, she just ran.

She had supposed that her friend was following behind. The truth was, she had experienced the age old 'fight or flight', and boy had she flown away, as fast as she had ever moved in her whole life.

She stood now, panting, her chest burning from the effort. She bent over and put her hands on her knees, trying to get a second wind. Her stomach was in agony, and she could feel that the stress of the situation had made her monthly bleeding heavier.

A long, screeching howl rang out through the trees, seeming to come from everywhere at once.

'Oh my God,' she wailed, 'fuck, fuck, *fuck*!'

She felt a wave of desperation hit her, and despite flaming lungs, legs that felt like jelly and the worst period pains she had ever experienced, she began to blindly run.

Smack.

Cursing as she tripped over something on the forest floor, Becky searched for the culprit in anguish. Her hand had landed in something soft and wet.

What the—

Becky screamed.

FELICITY HEARD A LOW, guttural growl. Quickly followed by a scream in the distance.

Bex!

The growling seemed to be coming from the mass of trees just behind her.

She jumped to her feet, wincing in pain as she put her

weight down on her twisted ankle. But she knew she had to run, or at least move as fast as she possibly could, away from whatever was lurking, ready to attack at any time.

She hobbled into the dense, wooded area right in front of her. She had no idea where she was now or how to get back to the camp; but she didn't care. She had to keep moving and try her very best to lose the thing behind her. She could only pray right now that somehow Becky had made it to the car, found Loz.

However, Felicity now realised *she* had the backpack with the keys in it.

She needed to make it to the 4x4, to save herself and her best friends.

The light was beginning to fade rapidly. Dusk was drawing in, and without daytime to guide her, she would be screwed. In desperation, she tried to blink away the tears as they were impairing what little vision she still had, but she was now weeping. She had never before felt so frightened, and utterly alone.

Becky choked back another scream.

Oh my God, oh my God!

Her mind was trying to make sense of it all. To process what she was seeing. To put a name to what she had tripped over.

There was so much blood it was hard to tell. But amongst the carnage, one thing stood out.

Rainbow coloured tie-dye.

Keep moving, Felicity thought in desperation, trying to ignore the agonising pain in her ankle.

She steadied herself against a tree, then froze in place as she sensed something behind her. Now, paralyzed as she was with fear, a raw charnel stench almost overpowered her. She could feel hot, fetid breath on the back of her neck.

Then, it snarled.

'Fu—'

'Ckk-hmff!' She managed to make a strangled groan as her face hit the mud, burying most of her mouth in its dark and claggy substance.

She was petrified. In her utter panic, she was struggling to breathe. Trying to lash out, she realised something had pinned her to the floor.

In terror, she felt her bladder betray her.

She could hear the low growl, feel the trembling of the putrid body on top of hers. It was strong; she had tried to move, but it was far too large and heavy. She began to wish the mud might suffocate her as it would be a far less painful death than whatever this horrific beast was about to do to her.

But mercy was not on her side. With one fell swoop it turned her over, pinning her arms by her side to keep her grounded. She was now face to face with the most petrifying thing that she had ever laid eyes on. It was, indeed, some sort of 'fucked-up wolf-man'. Its eyes glowed bright yellow and its fetid, rank, steaming breath came straight from a mouth full of the sharpest and meanest looking fangs she could have ever imagined.

She let out a blood-curdling shriek and the creature answered by howling with all its might, right into her face. It was the single most harrowing noise she had ever heard.

Oh God, she prayed, *please, just let it be quick.*

As if sensing her defeat, the creature then did something which disturbed her even further, although she wouldn't have imagined it could get any worse ...

It grinned at her.

Felicity could feel vomit rising in her throat, as it seemed to move its head down towards her crotch. She began to recall what Becky had been saying, about animals being attracted to menstrual blood and wanting to fuck her. She started to panic again. Was she about to be raped by this *thing*?

No. It just sniffed around her womanly area, rubbing its nose against her, but not seeming to want to try anything sexual. It peered up at her again, and this time, she could swear it seemed frustrated.

It seemed to notice the backpack, which was lying on the floor where it had fallen as the creature had pounced on her. It sniffed the bag, making a low rumbling, growling noise like an angry dog guarding its master. The pack was slightly open, and she could see some of Becky's supplies had spilled out onto the floor, including a wrapper with the used tampon inside.

It then stared back at her.

And smiled.

An actual fucking smile.

Seemed to take something, although she couldn't imagine what.

And then, raising one of its enormous paws, it swiped at her stomach with its razor-sharp claws.

Let out a howl of pure rage.

And then, in a flash, it was gone.

BECKY WAS by now completely wild with full blown terror and panic. She scuttled away from the remains of Loz, trembling all over. Bile rose in her throat as she shook her head from side to side.

'No, no, no,' she repeated over and over, like a small child refusing to believe they had actually seen the monster in the closet.

Darkness was falling and she had literally no idea where on earth she was or how to find her friend. She was dying for a cigarette and realised in an all-encompassing moment of utter gut-wrenching despair that she no longer had the backpack. Not only did that mean no fags or tampons, even more vital to her survival right now was the fact that if she ever found the fucking car, she didn't even have the keys.

BY NOW, it was almost dark. Felicity knew she must get up and move, in case it came back. She was in a state of shock and knew that she was in a very bad way. But somehow, a sense of survival also kicked in and that meant movement and trying to get back to the car, back to her friends.

She groaned in agony as she sat up. She could see the huge tear in her shirt and blood oozing through. Gingerly, she lifted it to survey the damage.

She choked back vomit. The creature had ripped open her stomach with its talons. There was a gaping wound, and she could see what appeared like part of her intestine poking out. But it had left her alive. Just. She reached over to grab Becky's bag. There were some emergency sanitary towels and she used them now to plug up the wound. It wouldn't last for long, but at least it would stem some of the bleeding whilst she tried to make her getaway. She needed to leave the scene of her attack, now.

Felicity, blinded by the dark and in agony, attempted to ready herself for her journey. She began to wonder about the wolf-man sniffing at her crotch, and then at the backpack with the tampons. Was that what had attracted it?

'Oh, Bex,' she cried, 'where are you?' She knew that her oldest friend was to be the creature's prize and somehow it would stop at nothing until it had her.

It was pitch black now.

Bam.

Becky had hit something large and very solid.

Yes! Oh, thank you, God!

It was the car. She put her head against the door and wept. In that moment, it didn't matter that she couldn't drive it away. It was a much-needed beacon of hope.

'Where are you, Flick?' she wailed.

Crack.

She heard a noise behind her. A jingling sound. *Oh, oh yes!* Becky knew what that was, it was the blessed sound of the car keys. Felicity must have found her.

She began to cry again in sheer relief, waiting for her saviour.

'Oh, Flick, thank God, let's get the fuck out …'

She didn't even have time to turn around.

'Fel—' she gurgled, blood spurting from her mouth.

Then crumpled down to the floor as it drew out its fist from her insides.

THE FUCKED-UP wolf-man smiled and sniffed her. What a prize. Oh, that glorious smell. Thick, delicious menstrual blood. Always made females more fun to track.

Then, he picked up Becky's body and threw it in the trailer. He would indeed savour every inch of her later. Laughing, he opened the door, put the keys in the ignition and drove away …

<u>Epilogue</u>

Keep moving, moving, must keep moving, she thought.

Shit. She cursed as she stumbled into a low branch.

It was pitch black and she had long since lost any sense of direction. She could have been anywhere.

Another wave of absolute blinding agony hit her.

The pain from her stomach wound had made her almost delirious, fading in and out of consciousness.

Only the blind hope of finding Becky and Loz had kept her alive.

Until now.

Total and utter despair filled her with a wave of complete resignation.

This was it.

The End.

She couldn't, *wouldn't* fight it anymore.

It was inevitable now. She was beyond exhausted, totally disorientated. And she was hurt. A fatal wound. She wasn't sure how long it took to bleed to death, but she knew she couldn't have long left.

'I'm sorry,' Felicity croaked. She lay there, on the ground, shaking, shivering, dying.

'We should never have come', she whispered, putting both of her hands onto her stomach, feeling the warm, wet, sticky oozing.

Snap.

With the very last of her strength, she managed to raise her eyes.

Whimpered...

It was standing right in front of her, grinning. Around one long, taloned finger, it spun something small, silver and shiny.

The car key.

He WHISTLED as he dragged her body back to his lair. He'd be full tonight.

Smiling, he climbed the tree and added the latest trophy to his collection.

The End.

Notes

You know we had a global pandemic in 2020, yeah? You remember that? Well, a bunch of UK horror writers banded together to form an anthology called *Diabolica Britannica* to raise money for the NHS. Somehow, I was invited to join and before I knew it, Adam Nevill and Tim Lebbon were on board and Ramsey Campbell was writing the foreword. And yes, that was a real WTF moment for sure.

I knew this book would likely be seen by many people due to those guys alone, so I needed to bring my A Game. *Footsteps* had originally been written set in the Pacific Northwest and there was more inference of actual wolf sightings. When I moved it to the UK for this anthology, I had to tweak that plotline. It still worked I think, as the main narrative revolved around menstruation no matter what country it took place in.

The main inspiration behind it isn't hard to determine. I'd recently watched *The Ritual* and the scene with the body displayed in the trees had stuck with me. I had also intended it to have a *Blair Witch* vibe. And of course, with the whole menstruation plot, there was even going to be a character called *Carrie*, but I ended up thinking that might be a bit too on the nose rather than an homage. I plucked Becky and Loz out of thin air, but Felicity is named for my daughter, even if she'll likely never read this.

I have since been told that it reminded people of both *Dog Soldiers* and *The Descent*. This may have been a subconscious tribute, since it is not a coincidence that they are two of my all-time favourite movies.

I have always been proud of this tale, and never more so than when I discovered it had been nominated for a 2020 Splatterpunk Award. I hope that you dug it too.

TRACK TWO

*J*ill - *The author must have been experimenting with her voice in this next story. It is quite unlike the others in both content and style, but nevertheless, is unmistakably her creation. Judging by the date, it is one of the earliest pieces, and almost akin to a folktale.*

A stark reminder that one should never trust a stranger, no matter how beguiling their smile.

Number 2 - When Doves Cry.

WIPING AWAY A SOLITARY TEAR, she realised in despair that darkness had begun to fall. Shivering, she drew her cloak tighter, for it had begun to rain. Carriages clattered past, hooves churning up the humble roads: the wealthy being transported warm and dry. Cursing under her breath, she made note of her surroundings. She did not know this city, having only arrived that evening. A meagre amount of money lined her pockets; she had not eaten in a while. The tattered cloak kept in little heat. It would be dangerous to stay out alone much longer with the street lighting so dim.

As she walked head down through the mist, she neared an inn. She paused to peer in through the frosted glass, seeing a large crackling fire and contented patrons partaking of their ale. She hesitated for just a moment. Then, upon hearing a loud clap of thunder overhead, she pushed open the door with trepidation. The blessed warmth was instantaneous and, heartened by the merriness, she was drawn further into the tavern by the flickering furnace. A scruffy wolfhound bounded over, wagging its tail. She remembered her dogs at home and was wrought with melancholic musings. *No*, she scolded. That was in the past and there it must stay.

A kindly looking gentleman approached her, taking a hold of the beast.

"My sincerest apologies, Mademoiselle," he purred, and she regarded his foreign sounding accent with interest, and just a little fear. "He is most fond of beautiful strangers. I hope that he did not cause you any alarm?"

"Not at all, Sir," she answered, trying not to look directly at the gentleman, although she could not help but notice how very handsome he was in his fine attire.

"Have you travelled far?" he enquired, his gaze falling on her small travelling bag.

"A long way," she replied, imbued with rue, yet feeling herself becoming less inhibited by the kindness he was showing.

"Then let me welcome you to these parts by asking you to join me for supper."

This was most bold. She had to remind herself she was

in the city now and ways were different, more modern. But still, she was reticent and did not want to appear forward.

"I wish to be no trouble, Sir," she answered, blushing. His mouth twitched, the suggestion of a smile, and she was struck by how kind and honest the gesture was.

"Go sit by the fire and warm your poor bones. I shall order bread and cheese. The broth here is the finest for miles."

She took her place by the hearth as instructed, thrilled at once by the heat that touched her. When the handsome stranger returned, he was accompanied by a ruddy-faced barmaid who placed their supper on the table. Casting her eyes downward, she was unable to swallow for a moment. She wasn't used to such kindness from a stranger and was unsure how to respond, yet as her soft belly rumbled she knew she wouldn't resist.

"This is far too generous, Sir. I do not know how I shall be able to repay my thanks." Her voice caught a little before she continued. "I have been left with very little and wonder how I shall survive before finding work." The gentleman smiled again, and the genuineness behind it made her feel hopeful that all in her world was not yet lost.

"My dear Mademoiselle, I am a man of wealth, yet I have no one to welcome into my home for this is not my place of birth. It is most fortuitous that I have room enough for you to be able to retire comfortably at my dwelling, and there will be no charge. It will be enough to have another being in the house that knows more than just to bark."

Her cheeks grew pink as she allowed his words to digest. Lowering her eyes, she reiterated not wishing to be any trouble. He laughed, insisting it was indeed no trouble at all, that she simply *must* accompany him home, and so she agreed. Although she was sure that it was not the *done* thing, she had no other choice but the freezing outdoors for company. At least there was no one left to think badly of her. No one at all.

As she was devouring the bread and cheese and marvelling at the wonderful taste of the broth, she noticed an oddity. The gentleman did not remove his gloves as he ate, and his movement was a tad stunted. She thought it strange, but not knowing much of the customs of the rich, and especially the foreign, it did not play on her mind for long. There was something about him, something almost feminine in his movement, although she could not quite place it.

Soon she grew weary, and the gentleman, seeming to notice, announced a carriage was waiting outside. The hound trotted beside them, escorting them to their ride. The driver carried her meagre bag and helped her into the coach.

Then, they were on their way...

'Twas a short journey, and soon they had reached their destination. The large building loomed, and for some reason she shivered as she glanced through the window of the coach. However, as the rain pounded on the roof and the storm continued to brew yet still, she was glad of having a room to rest in. The stranger led her into the vast premises as a manservant ensured the candles were lit and lamps were burning. Her cheeks flamed as she wondered what the help must think of her. The gentleman led her to the parlour and enquired as to whether she would join him for tea so he could, if he may, discover a little more about her.

She smiled with gratitude and smoothed her skirts in order to rest upon the couch. The hound came to lie beside her, and a young maid busied herself at the hearth, tending to the embers of the fire and lighting a new one. Once again, she revelled in the warmth, allowing it to seep into her bones. The gentleman remained standing, one hand resting upon the colossal stone fireplace. Another maid bustled in, laden down with the tea tray. As she poured from an ornate pot into two delicate china cups, there was a knock. His brow furrowed as he turned to answer.

Head bowed, the manservant appeared, announcing there was a messenger at the door requesting to see the master. The stranger excused himself apologetically and promised to return forthwith. In the meantime, he insisted she make herself at home; rest by the fireplace and enjoy her tea. Both maids followed, and so she was left on her lonesome.

As the door closed, she was overcome with curiosity and began to wander about the parlour whilst supping the warming nectar. There was another door leading to the library, and beyond that what appeared to be a study.

She glanced around with surreptitiousness, knowing she should not enter, but intrigue overpowered common sense. She gasped in wonder as she entered the study, for it was filled with the finest furniture and most wonderous paintings. A large globe adorned his desk and a beautiful cabinet with ornate carvings was the centrepiece of it all. It drew her in, and on nearing she noted the carvings were most perplexing. Perhaps, they might be Egyptian or Greek, although she could not say for sure. The cabinet emitted a peculiar warning as if forbidding her to touch. The feeling was overwhelming, yet one she could not resist. Setting down the teacup, she floated over to the nebulous object.

As she pried apart its huge doors, there was dread in the

pit of her belly. It swung open and a scream rose in her throat.

Inside, carefully strung like a necklace, was a piece of string. Swinging from the woven chain were two human thumbs and seven fingers. The room began to spin as nausea ensued, and she fought the urge to vomit or fall faint. Hands shaking, she closed the doors with great care and backed away from the monstrosity she had witnessed. Chest hitching and dinner churning in her belly, her mind tried in desperation to process what she had seen.

She tiptoed towards the parlour, careful not to make a sound. She would wait for her host to reappear, then make her excuses to leave before the monster she had trusted like the fool she was could discover what she now knew. But before she could reach the doorway, a hand clamped onto her shoulder.

He had returned, the beguiling smile vanished.

"Curiosity is not a becoming characteristic for a young lady," He growled, pushing her back into the study and slamming the door behind them. "I had been tempted to keep you as my pet, save you from your intended fate. But now my dear, you have left me no choice."

Sighing, he took her hand, stroking it like a cat. "Still, at last it will be complete. It is something that I have yearned for, for many years."

Her mind was thick. She felt sleepy and slumped into a chair, confused by what was happening. She regarded the manservant who had joined them. The cabinet was open and empty. The fingers had been removed and were now placed upon his desk. They had been positioned into the shape of two hands, only the right had the little finger missing ...

Removing his gloves, he revealed the grotesque stumps

where digits should have been. The fingers of the gloves had been stuffed with clay, to give the false impression of being 'normal'.

Something glistened, its shiny surface reflecting the light from the candles...a knife.

"You have such pretty hands, Mademoiselle," the gentleman cooed, his smile having returned. "Perfect for the final 'taking'."

Needle and thread lay next to the severed digits, and she began to realise even through her drugged state what was about to happen.

"Of course, it is a shame you have to die, but this must never get out. I am sure that you understand, n'est pas?"

The blade came first to her smallest phalange, and then to her throat. She was not even able to scream.

NOWADAYS, the gentleman removes his gloves whilst dining. There are still some scars, but they have healed well in the circumstances. He is often complimented for his aristocratic, feminine fingers. He spends much of his time in the inns of the countryside, where the poorer folk and weary travellers tend to gather. When it is dry, patrons often dance about, barefoot on the straw covered floors. He is always on the lookout for a lonesome young lady...the one with the prettiest toes.

The End.

Notes

The original version of this story, which isn't far off what you read today, was hand-written on the balcony of a tiny hotel room in Corfu in 2000. My then boyfriend, now husband and I were on our first holiday together during the summer before our third year at Uni. It was the cheapest get-away we could afford, and we loved it. Something about the cool blue sea and the brilliant sunshine brought out the dormant writer within. I had taken a couple of literacy electives during my second year and regained some of the buzz for writing that hadn't surfaced for a few years as exams and Law had taken over. Something about being in that 'olde worlde' Mediterranean village brought out my creative side, and I scribbled this yarn out in a couple of hours, pencil furiously whisking across the paper as I fought to get all the ideas down before they upped and left again.

I'm not sure I even thought about this story again until the last couple of years when I happened upon it. At some point, I had transcribed it onto the PC and printed it out. After playing around a little, implementing grammatical structures I had learnt since its fruition, the tale was ready to be shared.

You'll note it could be gothic, maybe quiet horror, with its subtlety and inference rather than full on gore and violence of my latter work. Still, it holds a special place in my heart, so I hope you enjoyed it.

TRACK THREE

Jill - This seemed rather intriguing; you don't often stumble across split narrative in such short stories. It certainly speaks to her specific influences. I can't say too much without giving anything away, but I could tell she had fun.

Yet another 'all is not as it may seem' scenario, read along to find out just who she is and who is holding her captive...

Number 3 - I Want to Break Free

Part One - Her

She was trying not to panic, but it wasn't easy. Rotating her stiff neck, she wondered yet again how long she'd been held captive. Had days now turned into weeks?

She'd stopped trying to keep count as it had been a pointless task, each day seamlessly blending into another.

Time didn't seem to exist and the days were but a blur. With no windows in the room to enlighten her of the sun rising and setting, she had no sense of the hour.

She had been fed – a meagre offering, but still - and was allowed to rest. Whether these meals were at regular intervals or simply at random, she had no way of knowing.

Not that it even mattered.

Exercise was occasionally permitted, which boiled down to walking the length of her chains in circles around the chair she spent most of her time bound to.

In the beginning, she had alternated between screaming and sobbing with gusto. Bruised vocal cords and dehydration had soon put a stop to that. Now, she was silent.

There was a bucket to relieve herself when necessary. The stench of piss and shit was now so familiar that she didn't even flinch when it remained full for hours on end.

Torment had kept her motivated, endless torture thinking about her family. How distraught they must be.

She pushed the memories away now, wanting to keep her head clear. The pain had been too intense, too draining. What little strength she had left needed to be harnessed.

Sporadically, she would feel the intense need to vomit. Thank God that stage had lessened as there was so little within her to purge.

At least her wounds appeared to be healing. That had been one of her many fears, that the gaping holes in her torso would get infected, turn septic. A slow agonising infliction of pain as her own body poisoned her from within.

But at least for the moment, they seemed less angry. Which was ironic since she was seething, a burning ball of furious flames waiting to erupt.

She was no longer bothered by the silence. Aside from

the rattling of her chains and the occasional clunk as the door opened and food was brought in, noise was scarce.

Now, a new and unwelcome sound brings on the panic: the tightness in her chest, worms in her belly.

Because it is so very different from the clinical thumps and bangs of her prison.

This sounds...alive.

Yes.

There it is again.

This noise emanates from a 'something'. She is certain of it.

Her eyes widened. Why? Why was someone else here?

Through the paper-thin walls, she can hear the howling screams of extreme pain and pure and utter terror from the other side.

She groans, the first noise she has made in days. Why were they doing this? If they were going to kill her then for fuck's sake why were they keeping her hostage?

She begins twisting her body in the chair. The chains are tight today so she cannot get much traction, but she is able to wriggle to and fro a bit.

She yells, more in frustration than pain, "Let me the fuck out of here!"

Imbued with rage, her fight returns in spades. How dare they keep her captive here? The more riled up she becomes, the more her face turns puce, mouth frothing. She shrieks as loud as her injured throat will allow; the inhuman wail akin to a possessed banshee.

"Let me out!"

She stops.

The door is opening...just a crack.

The smell is immediate and overwhelms her in an instant.

Blood.

So.

Much.

Blood.

Screaming, hissing - she is a wild animal. She snarls and throws herself around in her chair as much as the chains will allow. They are chafing and cutting into her, but she does not give a flying fuck now.

Roaring, the beast within ready to pounce, "Get me out of here!"

Behind the door, she senses movement.

Her eyes bulge in fear. Shock.

The beast quells as she sees Him.

She smells the blood. She practically tastes it. And she sure as hell now sees it.

Grinning, the man waves about the severed head he is holding.

She sucks in her breath, trying as hard as she can, although it's impossible, to shrink back into the walls and escape the inevitable.

Her fate.

She thinks he is mocking her, licking his lips.

She tries in desperation to compose herself. She does not want to give him the satisfaction of seeing just how terrified she is, and how very hungry.

He waves the head at her. "Dinner?" he asks with a glint in his eye.

In a regular hunt, in usual circumstances, there would not be a chance in hell she would eat...that.

And he knows it. But right now, she is so starving, so

needy, that even the decapitated noggin of a werewolf looks pretty damn tasty.

She knows it might kill her.

Vampires should never feed on other demons. Only humans. It doesn't always harm them, but it was like Russian Roulette. You never knew which particular Blood Line one was from.

The man is taunting her. And enjoying it.

She continues to scream and struggle against her restraints. By now, one of her wrists is broken, the bone protruding through her skin, but she doesn't even notice. Her need to feed is so strong that she would have bitten her own arm off to get to that head.

Seeing her captor approach, she fills with bloodlust and her beast releases.

She snarls, teeth bared like a rabid wolf. More irony.

She watches him bring the foul dog meat closer to her. She is about to tear through her chains to not only feast on that disgusting flea-bitten mongrel, but to also savour every damn moment of draining the man of his blood and soul.

She fails to notice when, quick as a flash, he whips a stake out from behind his back and pounds it straight into her sunken chest, penetrating right into her fetid, blackened heart.

THE HUNTER SMILES. They had kept her longer than usual. Long enough for one of her family to come looking, so they were able to follow him back to The Nest. And kill them all.

He wipes the stake clean on the leg of his trousers.

Then, he puts down his trophy with care and claims a second.

. . .

Part Two - Him

The act itself had been simple, having succeeded many times before. He was well practiced, had done his homework. It would be foolish to just grab someone off the street and keep them prisoner without planning and preparation. There was procedure to follow.

Of course, this was not his first rodeo. He had plenty of scars to prove it.

This one however could prove to be profitable, lucrative even.

Licking his lips at the anticipation, he revelled in the excitement. This part was always the most thrilling, satisfactory to his needs.

The buzz from the potential danger of the kidnap was wavering. Adrenaline was lowering.

That needed fixing.

Now, it was time for some fun.

He could hear her screaming.

Let the games begin.

The noise abated at last. Her chest hitched with a few shuddering sobs, but at least that god-awful din had subsided.

Glancing at his watch, he noted twelve hours or so had passed since he had brought her here. Tied her up with chains.

She'd been hurt pretty bad. Her fault for struggling so

much. She was a fighter. At first, anyway. He'd relished her pain. Bitch deserved it.

But for now, at least, he needed her alive. This would only work if her family believed that.

So, he took a bucket into the room for her and some food. *He* wasn't the monster after all.

OVER THE NEXT couple of days, he stuck to the job at hand. Played by the rules. She now ceased to make any noise at all. She was slumped over in the chair, the chains rubbing against her lacerations, and he noticed the larger wounds seemed to be healing. He might have considered it quite remarkable, had he not been utterly repulsed.

Approaching the chair, regarding her weakened state, he loosened the chain around her feet, just a little. This allowed exercise, and more importantly, gave her hope. He took great pleasure in that.

He darted back, but she didn't even flinch.

Later, at 'feeding' time, he'd return. He chuckled to himself at the notion.

IT TOOK a while (much longer than he would have liked), but the family finally made contact. One of her brothers came snooping around and made the rest of the job a piece of cake. There is no feeling in the world quite like it. Nothing comes close, not even the best fuck you've ever had.

He had achieved his goal; he got what he had wanted. The nest was no more. And found a little bonus on the way back too, something to play with. A twofer!

Getting it back to the holding place had not been quite as simple as before. This one wanted to fight and struggle the *whole* time, no let up. Still, it made it more of a challenge, something exciting and intense. He liked that. God, he liked that a lot.

It was easier once he managed to get to the cell next to her. Bitch was still silent.

He would not bother with chains and a chair for this one, as there was no need to keep it alive. This had been for the sheer hell of it, the thrill of the hunt. The exhilaration.

Now came his favourite part. The Kill.

But he did not want this death to be quick and painless. There needed to be suffering, screaming. Sounds of agonised torment.

And something a little bit extra, just for him.

A deep thrust.

Guttural moans.

Bodily fluids spurting everywhere.

This was what he lived for.

Whilst finishing off, he heard what he had been waiting for.

Screeching and then, "Let me the fuck out of here!"

Banging and rattling as she struggled against her restraints. Oh yes, she was almost ready.

There was blood *everywhere*. So much, thick and coppery. He knew she must be able to smell it. It would be driving her insane.

Smiling, he closed the door, holding his prize in one hand, and made his way towards her.

SHE IS ROARING in pure animal-like rage now.

He pushes her door ajar.

She freezes.

There is sheer unadulterated terror and shock plastered all over her disgusting face.

She sees his prize.

He licks his lips and winks, imagining it to be seductive.

And waves the severed wolf head at her.

"Dinner?" he asks, mocking.

He can see the bloodlust and hunger in her eyes. He knows she is torn, but she is starving.

She howls with desire and begins what seems to be the process of trying to break her own bones to get out of the restraints. The only thing that matters now is feeding.

She is baring her blackened teeth, foul stinking spittle drooling down her chin.

Oh yes, *this* is the best part.

He knows that in normal circumstances she would never even entertain a werewolf as dinner, and that makes it all the sweeter. He sees the inner turmoil etched on her face. Lycan blood is abhorrent, but she is so fucking hungry…

He approaches with care, the revolting, thick dog blood dripping from the tendons left dangling from the hasty decapitation and reads the rabid look in her eyes. Oh yes, not only is she dying to rip the fetid head from his hand and sink her teeth into it, but she also wants to tear him limb from limb. Suck him dry.

For a fleeting moment, he considers taunting her a little longer, but knows that even with his much-notched belt, it would now be way too risky.

He withdraws the stake from his back pocket and, quick as a flash, with pristine aim and expertise, pierces it straight into her un-dead, blackened heart.

He experiences the usual euphoria, ecstasy akin to the greatest pleasurable release.

Stepping back to peruse his work, he smiles.

"Another one bites the dust."

The Hunter wipes the stake clean on the leg of his trousers and places the lycanthrope's noggin onto the floor.

He unsheathes the silver hunting knife he keeps on his belt and claims his second trophy of the day.

The End.

Notes

The idea for this was simple. I had read a short noir about a girl who is held hostage for ransom and uses her feminine wiles to manipulate her capture. Of course, I have yet to dabble in that particular genre, so my mind went straight to creature and hunter – I truly blame my love of *Supernatural*.

I then thought it might be fun to mix it up a little by doing a split POV. I enjoy longer work where each chapter represents a different character. It is a cool way to see into both thought processes without too much head hopping.

It makes you wonder who the real monster is...

TRACK FOUR

Jill - I wonder whilst reading through more of the stories, if she had any links to the police? Maybe she was once a serving officer? They seem to appear in more than one of her works. I must look at the casefile when I get back to the office. This was another tale with a twist, which seems to be one of her minor trademarks. Not every narrative needs it, but it is often fun, especially if you don't see it coming. If I say anymore, I might give something away.

Number 4 - Maneater

BLOOD.

Pure delicious, sweet, sweet blood.

Never tired of it.

And now, there was finally a way to satisfy the constant, raging thirst...

Detective Cameron Anders rubbed his hands over his face, his expression one of resignation. The scene was all too familiar.

Three bodies.

Two shot at close range. One female, two males.

Well, he assumed the third was male from the clothing. There wasn't much of *his* face left to be sure. He was still clutching the weapon, a sawed-off shotgun and the cause of the hole where his head should have been.

It smacked of a classic murder-suicide, but with one unusual difference. All three victims had been exsanguinated. Not a single drop of blood remained.

His partner came closer to him, nose wrinkling in disgust as she shuffled in the forensics suit worn to keep the scene intact.

Detective Kate Ramsey was pissed.

"How many more before we catch a break on this?" she asked. "This guy has got to be the most prolific serial killer the state has ever had!"

Gesturing at the bodies, she added, "And the most fucked up. Where in hell's teeth is the goddamn blood?"

She shook her head in frustration, muttering under her breath and storming off.

Sighing in submission, Cameron conceded they were done; it was up to the CSIs now to take care of collecting the evidence.

He joined Kate outside, where she was angrily inhaling a cigarette.

"What do we got so far?" he enquired.

"Not a lot. Meth heads. Looks like the perp caught their

dealer and his lady hooking up." She shrugged her shoulders. "I'm sick to death of this shit!"

She threw the cigarette butt on the floor, stamping on it with vigour. She was an excellent detective, and he knew she'd harness that rage. They just needed to get away from the carnage.

He opened the squad car door and gestured for her to get in, which she did, albeit begrudgingly. Her radio crackled as she sat down, and she gave him the stink eye, as if he were somehow in control of dispatch now too.

Deciding upon a childish approach to break her out of the stupor, he stuck his tongue out and blew a raspberry. The move had the desired effect, and she laughed and shook her head. "Come on then, loser. Let's do some more digging back at the ranch."

"I JUST DON'T FUCKING GET it, argh!" Kate slammed a fist onto the desk and then took a long gulp of strong, black coffee. "I know the CSIs are working their asses off on this. But where the fuck is the blood?"

Cameron looked at his partner, chewing the end of his pencil, deep in thought.

"The kill scene must be somewhere else. It doesn't make a lick of sense for a whole body's worth of fluid to be missing. It's the only thing that seems plausible."

They had spent a long day going over and over the crime scene and comparing it to the others. The killing spree had been going on for months now. With an ever-increasing body count they knew the Feds would be breathing down their necks soon enough. The pressure was inevitable; it was a matter of *when*, not if.

Cameron read Kate's mood and knew it was pointless trying to get anything else done now. They'd hit the proverbial wall. Deciding to call it a day, he suggested they go home, rest, and come back in the morning with fresh eyes.

He relied on the unexplored sexual tension he believed to be present between them. He knew his partner better than anyone, could predict her reaction.

And as always, she took the bait.

CAMERON'S RELIEF WAS PALPABLE; he was beyond tired.

As he was driving home to his out-of-town apartment, he spotted a car with plates he recognised. It had been used in a child molestation case, and he was pretty sure it still had an active BOLO.

He tailed it with caution for a short time, not calling it in just yet. The vehicle slowed as it neared some woods. He turned off his lights so as not to be seen, his suspicion mounting. Watching with care, he saw a man exit the car and head to the rear. Cameron put his hand to his hip, reassured by the presence of his service pistol. Although his line of sight was now slightly obscured, he could see the male open the trunk, pull something out, and carry it in his arms into the woods.

Cameron exited his car using stealth. He pulled his radio, which was active but set to mute, from the glove compartment and followed the suspect into the forest.

Now, he could see what the man was holding, and could tell the child was dead.

Despite years of experience, and many previous cases just as abhorrent, a cop never gets over finding a dead kid. Rage took over common sense and procedure as Cameron fought the urge to race over and rip this motherfucker a new one.

But something stopped him, spoke to his cop's intuition, and told him to stand by. And, as per usual, that second sight was correct: another figure was stepping out of the darkness. Craning to see who the newcomer was, Cameron listened with intent, waiting for his chance to rush out and clip the pair of dirty bastards.

Along with the second voice came a sense of recognition and confusion. He could only suppose it was some kind of honeytrap that he'd not been privy too, despite the unlikelihood. Yes, it had to be. Any other reason was incomprehensible. He'd wait just a moment and then rush in as back up.

And then it happened.

Even with the coppery tang in the air, followed by the nauseating stench of shit, his mind wouldn't process the scene unravelling before him. He closed his eyes and pressed his hands, one still holding the now useless gun, over his ears, yet he could still hear the gurgling and glugging.

He shook his head like a kid refusing to believe it was bedtime and then...an unmistakable thud hitting the ground.

It was done.

A lone whimper escaped his lips as he sensed rather than saw the presence next to him. The blood must have given her some sort of super-human strength, as she was able to wrench him from his crouching position with ease.

"Look. At. Me." She hissed, placing emphasis on each word.

He didn't want to. He willed his eyes to stay shut but knew that sooner or later he would have to face the facts.

Standing so close he could smell the blood on her

breath, he opened his eyes and was greeted with a sight that would never leave him, if he were to survive.

The thing resembled Kate, but any sense of humanity within her eyes was gone, replaced by bloodlust. Then there were her teeth or, to be more accurate, her fangs, which were dripping blood like a leaky faucet. In fact, her entire lower jaw was scarlet and it ran onto her clothing, giving her the appearance of a contender on Man v. Food, only this was Kate v. Paedo-douchebag.

At this point, he wasn't sure if the stench of shit and piss was emanating from the deceased blood donor or himself, his bladder and bowels emptying and adding to his discomfort. Yet, as terrified as he was and certain of his imminent demise, he saw the crimson leave her eyes and the original 'sky on a summer's day' hue return. Even more vital at this stage was the retraction of her fangs. She was still covered in blood, but the immediate threat to his life appeared to have lessened.

His heartbeat began to return to a regular pace, and he managed to open his mouth to speak, hoping actual words would appear and not remain stuck to his vocal cords.

"Kate, wha-"

Of course, he didn't get to finish his question. The vamp may have retracted but *she* wasn't a fucking idiot.

SHE WATCHED with apathy as her partner's body slumped down the tree he had been resting against, the gaping hole in his head leaving a distinct track of viscera and brain matter. Shame she was no longer hungry; she didn't like to waste a meal.

The euphoria from the feed had dissipated and she was

able to think straight. Having worn gloves as always, prints weren't an issue. And she was so light on her feet there was no trail of footprints. Using Cameron's revolver, Kate shot the waste-of-space-kiddie-fiddler in the chest and head. It would look more like a paedo-revenge killing now. It had been fortuitous he'd felt the need to bring a gun to the party, which she now placed back into his dead hand.

She didn't touch the child. Even monsters have standards, and she absolutely never fed on kids. Not even dead ones.

Walking back to the car parked at the opposite end of the woods, she may have experienced something akin to sorrow for the inevitable dog walker who would find the remains in the morning, if she had been able to feel such emotions.

It was ironic that she and Cameron would be called to attend, unless the patrol officer who responded thought to check for ID. They'd never be able to tell from his non-existent face. The exsanguination would cause no end of puzzled frowns and scratched heads. She might even get compassionate leave; they'd been partners for years after all.

Kate sighed as she reached her car. At least another dirty, low life piece of shit was off the streets. Shame about Anders but he was collateral damage, and it wasn't as though she was capable of remorse. Afterall, she was dead and devoid of emotion. She might be able to act the part and react in an expected manner, drawing on memories of sentiments from long ago. She could cry, feign joy, rage, elation. But it was all an illusion, part of her cover. And she couldn't be discovered, not when there was still so much work to be done.

Becoming a cop was her best move yet in her little over five hundred years on this planet.

She got to feed and sate her bloodlust. But not on innocents. She moved from state to state, city to city, using expert skills honed as a homicide detective to glean insider information from cops and snitches alike.

The man in the woods had been her preferred choice of dinner. Having been a mother herself, many centuries ago, she still longed for children. But she would never sire, never force another to live this way.

Anyone who hurt and messed with kids, they were first on the menu. Drug dealers and those who ruined lives without a care in the world were also delicacies.

Detective Kate Ramsey actually believed she was helping. Even if occasionally, there was an unexpected hiccup.

Afterall, it was *she* who was ridding the world of monsters...

The End

Notes

I hadn't actually realised how many of my characters are police officers until someone asked me about it. I guess it comes from the old adage 'write what you know.' This wasn't created for any particular call or purpose, it just seemed like an entertaining story. And who doesn't like a bad-ass female vampire detective? My very good friend Cameron Chaney has a major part in a novella I must finish one day, but he needed to make an appearance in this collection as well. I just hope he doesn't mind being killed off...again.

TRACK FIVE

Jill - Some of the papers I found, have left me in two-minds as to whether I should share them. They seem a little more risqué than the run-of-the-mill monster tales. This is one of those such works. Don't say I didn't give you warning.

Number 5 - Addicted to Love.

"I THINK you're really fucking gorgeous," the woman shouted into his ear, no doubt spraying a shit load of saliva all over the side of his face too. *Thanks, love.* Still, she did need to shout to have a chance in hell of being heard above Wham.

Pasting on a smile, he nuzzled into her neck and replied with as much gusto but less bodily fluid, "No, *you* are the gorgeous one."

Despite it being the oldest line in the book, and not even a very good one, the umpteen vodkas the woman had knocked back made this seem like the most hilarious thing she had ever heard.

She burped then snorted, bringing her face closer to his and rubbing her remarkable chest up against him.

"So, if I'm so gorgeous, what you gonna do about it, hmm?" One eye was twitching, just enough to indicate she may not be one hundred percent compos mentis.

Donnie smiled, the cat that got the cream. Looking at her impressive cleavage, he made her an offer he knew she wouldn't refuse. Frankie Goes to Hollywood began playing, which he felt was most fortuitous.

"How about we get a cab back to my place, and I shag you 'til you can't walk anymore?"

For a split second, he thought he saw a flash in her eye. Upon closer inspection he realized they were just glassy, and the drop of spittle that leaked from her lopsided grin gave him the answer he needed. As they left the club he nodded at the bouncer, who in turn smirked and wiggled his eyebrows. A non-verbal 'nice one, mate' or 'pwoar, someone's getting laid tonight".

The gods of luck were on his side as he saw an available taxi was waiting: engine idling, cabbie brooding, smoking and looking like he wished he was anywhere else.

Bingo.

He pushed the giggling woman into the vehicle and jumped in beside her. She was already trying to ram her tongue down his throat, and he barely managed to croak out, "Barringer Avenue please, mate," before he was pinned down and the snogging began in earnest.

The cabbie nodded and began fiddling with his fare machine when the female broke free and piped up with, "No!", and then clarified, "I mean, let's go to mine instead."

Then, stage whispering into his face, nose to nose, she

added, "I've got naughty stuff and you can stick it up my arse, yeah?" She collapsed into him in a fit of giggles.

What the fuck?

"Well," growled the cabbie, "where are we going?"

Now, the man had plans that he needed to be at his own place in order to execute. However, even without those special implements, his main aim was to get laid, and this poor cow was willing and eager to go a stage further. He usually had to coax them, work hard for anal. Now it was being handed to him on a plate!

Thinking with his dick, as men are often apt to do, he nodded with enthusiasm, indicating she should relay her address to the driver.

Hiccup.

"Kirkland Road, guvnor!" Then, disobeying all sorts of seat belt rules and regulations, she straddled him and kissed him hard and fast, hands moving to his now very hard cock. Goddamn it, if he wasn't careful, he was going to cum in his boxers before he was anywhere near her welcoming pussy or arsehole.

The taxi sped through a part of town he didn't know too well, finally pulling up outside a block of flats that looked as if they'd seen better days. Although he dressed down as to not attract gold diggers, the man was used to certain creature comforts that weren't always readily available on this side of the tracks. Still, he was here to fuck her, not marry her, so he would have to manage without the Egyptian cotton sheets or teasmade.

"Three quid, mate."

He tossed a fiver at the cabbie and flung himself out of the door, dragging her behind him. This might be her gaff, but he wanted her to know from the get-go this was still *his* game.

Donnie watched her fannying about with her handbag for a moment or two, one of those ridiculous affairs that don't look big enough to hold a packet of fags, let alone anything else. She found the key at last, but his impatience grew as she tried to insert it into the lock which must have appeared to her as though it were moving. A triumphant look appeared on her face as she located the hole, and he realised just how wasted she was. No matter, she was willing, and he was eager. Very, very eager.

As she led him up the stairs he took in the shape of her arse, all snug in the dress that had left almost nothing to the imagination. It made him think of those birds in that Robert Palmer video. Addicted to Love, was it? They were fucking gorgeous too. He was so hard now it was almost painful. They stood in front of an inner door that looked to have seen some action judging by the peeling paint - and was that a muddy boot print? – and then she was grabbing him towards her again, giving him a final preview of what was to come before opening the lock. This time she opened it with ease, although he was so horny, he failed to notice.

She flung her keys, bag and heels on the floor and pushed him up against the wall. Since all his blood was in his member, his brain neglected to remember that he liked to be in control and wasn't used to this female dominance. She tore the dress over her head in one fluid motion, releasing the heaving and bare breasts underneath he'd been ogling, and revealing, as he'd suspected, that she wore no knickers. He sucked on her nipples as she threw back her head, and he could smell her sex was ready. His fingers fumbled with his own shirt buttons and she again took over, undoing the zipper on his jeans with determination and finally releasing his throbbing cock.

"Ooooh goody," she giggled, reaching towards it with her

fingers yet stopping just before the shaft. She licked her lips and indicated she wanted to take him full in her mouth, and his eyes rolled back just a tad as he imagined his cum shooting down her throat.

"But not here. To the bedroom!" She hooked her fingers through his belt loop and drug him into her chambers. Pushing him now to the bed, she pulled off his jeans and boxers, the whole-time maintaining eye contact. It was a miracle he hadn't yet exploded. His arousal was working overtime and he wanted nothing more than to slide inside any one of her orifices, he was no longer bothered which.

She crawled onto the bed and made as if to straddle him. This was the reason he haunted those clubs with their terrible music and cheap, nasty booze.

Thank fuck, at last some pussy, but just as he could feel the heat and wetness of her sex hovering above his member, she seemed to think better of it, the fucking tease.

"One last thing," she said, "and it'll be worth it when you blow your load, promise."

She reached into the nightstand next to the bed and then waved something silver in front of him.

Handcuffs. Well okay. He wouldn't have guessed she was into kinky shit, but he was up for *anything* to release his swollen balls. To be honest, his own bag of tricks back at his place had a few items straight out of a bondage porno film, so he was into it.

She clicked them into place and ensured he was nice and secure, then gave him what he wanted at last.

Almost anyway.

For just a moment, she turned away from him, seeming to gyrate her hips whilst rubbing her ample breasts. He presumed she was getting herself wetter and that was A-OK with him. Facing back towards him, she continued tweaking her nipples, one hand straying towards her clit. He was panting now, gagging for it. Sashaying over, she leant down and placed each rock-hard nipple into his mouth at a time. He sucked furiously, like a babe suckling its mother's teat, getting closer and closer to his time to shine.

Then, crawling back on top of him, she faced the wall at the far end of the room so he could just see her toned back muscles before he closed his eyes in ecstasy and imagined her riding him like a cowgirl. She slid onto him, giving his cock some much needed fun and riding him until the point he was just about to explode...

One thing he had paid no attention to whatsoever was the flashing red dot up on the ceiling near the curtains. Nor had he noticed how the mattress was extra squeaky, as if there was plastic beneath the cheap, dark sheet. And had he realised she'd coated her nipples in a clear, tasteless liquid, he may not have been so keen to take them into his willing mouth.

She ripped away her pussy just as his body started to twitch, the orgasm nearing the point of no return, and turned to face him without straddling back on to his soaking cock.

"What the fuck are you doing?" he shouted, his balls screaming at the injustice. He couldn't even finish himself off since he was cuffed to the bed post.

He watched in hopeful confusion as she reached her hand under the bedframe and brought out something he wasn't used to seeing in these circumstances.

The pain didn't register at first.

His foggy mind was still in the throes of a potential release, so it was only when he saw the bone and gristle now protruding from where his ankle should have been that the agony engaged, and he let out a howl like an enraged, caged beast.

Before he could react in any other way, she slammed the hammer down onto the other leg, this time ripping through his shin bone, shattering it in an instant.

Screaming, he tried to bring his fist toward her, forgetting he was handcuffed. The metal chafed his wrist, causing another area of intense and immediate discomfort.

Through his tears he noticed her look towards a small, flashing red light on the ceiling and nod.

"Wh-what are you doing?" he managed to choke out between sobs of misery. Both his shin and ankle were broken, and he was now helpless, unable to defend himself. What the fuck had happened? One minute he was well on the way to O-town and now this?

His vision began to blur, eyelids twitching and drooping, and he wasn't sure if it was just a result of the pain or shock or something else. However, it was not impaired enough to miss her wielding that hammer, smashing it into his right cheekbone, shattering his jaw and eye socket. Moaning in anguish, he moved his head to one side to vomit up dinner, the few beers he'd allowed himself at the club and several of his teeth.

His blurry vision now down to just the one eye, he struggled to understand what was occurring around his midsection and genitals. She had something shiny, and now there was a lot of red and yellow and...sausages? Wait, oh god! He suddenly understood what was happening. The drugs he had ingested via sucking on those titties were keeping him alert, so he begged for death to be quick as it sure as fuck wasn't painless.

He couldn't be certain in the end if he choked on his own gore and vomit, or if his heart could no longer cope with the massive blood loss draining from his visceral epicentre.

THE WOMAN WAS WRIST deep in his guts when his heart gave up the ghost. She may have made a physical comparison to *Carrie*, if she'd ever seen it. She was still waiting for a VHS copy to rent.

She looked up at the camera and signalled it was over. End the tape.

She climbed off the male, whose abdomen had been ripped open in a crude fashion with the butcher's knife, and opened the en-suite door, intending to hit the shower whilst the cleaners turned up and did their thing. She wasn't shocked at the amount of red pooling in the shower tray, nor at the bits of fat, flesh and pubic hair that caught in the drain cover.

She would like to tell you that she was a survivor and preying on males who were obviously trying to get their leg over wasted girls was payback. But that simply wasn't true, and she was no caped avenger.

Maybe she was just trying to earn some cash to purchase black market medicine for a sick relative?

Nope.

Her abusive, pimp boyfriend forced her into it?

Not even close.

The truth of the matter was Kenzie liked to fuck and she liked to kill.

She may as well be paid to do it.

But only in that order. Anything else would just be...unseemly.

She wasn't a sicko.

The End.

Notes

The premise behind this story is plain and simple. I wanted to write about a snuff movie! Think *Mail Order* by Jack Ketchum or Kristopher Triana's *The Devouring* and you'll see my inspiration. I felt setting it in the 80s was perfect as the characters weren't encumbered with updating social media or texting. And the names are a nod to Donnie Goodman (sorry, man) and Kenzie Jennings, my splatterpunk BFF, who assisted unknowingly with the very end line.

TRACK SIX

Jill - Parts of this next story seemed very realistic; if she were ever to resurface, I'd want to know if any of this chilling tale was true.

What happens when a family revisits their childhood holiday home? Will any deep, dark secrets be revealed, or supressed memories come to light?

Number 6 - Sweet Child O Mine

Do you ever have random flashbacks from your childhood? Things that awaken certain memories. For me the smell of a certain plastic takes me right back to My Little Ponies, and the *Terminator 2* theme music will always evoke memories of kissing Edward Furlong posters...

But sometimes we bury stuff, and we keep it dormant. Maybe it was a test you failed, or that time you saw the neighbour's cat after it had been run over. We discard those memories and hide them in our subconscious. We might not even know why our mind has deemed it necessary to banish them. And sometimes, even without our permission, they come back.

A FEW MONTHS AGO, my parents asked if we would like to join them on a break at an old farmhouse we used to holiday at sometimes when I was a kid. It was right in the middle of Devon, and we used to love it there. They'd been back a few times since, but I hadn't personally returned since I was eleven. But since I now have a seven-year-old of my own, and we were having a year off from expensive international travel, my parents thought it might be nice to all stay in the countryside together. That way their granddaughter could experience some of the old-fashioned rural fun that I'd loved as a child.

And why not? My husband and I worked hard, and our daughter was so used to theme parks and exotic beach holidays that something like this might be just what we needed.

As we counted down the days, I had this nagging worry in my mind that I couldn't attribute an origin to. I'm often anxious before we travel, concerned I'll forget the passports or the travel money, so I put it down to that. But I couldn't shake that sense of trepidation.

One morning at work, whilst I was on a break from the busy courtroom, I decided to call my mum.

"Mum," I began, "when we used to stay at Meyer's Farm, did anything, well, bad ever happen?" To be honest, I felt stupid even asking. Here I was, resplendent in wig and gown, working on a nasty rape case and I was asking if I'd ever had a boo-boo as a child and forgotten about it.

Mum laughed. "No, my darling," she answered. "You absolutely adored the place. Couldn't wait to go back each year."

For some reason this failed to settle my nerves. Still, life was busy, and all too soon it was time for the drive down to Devon. Our daughter was beside herself with excitement, and my husband was looking forward to a few days away from the nick. Yet the closer we got to Meyer's Farm, the more anxious I felt. I didn't want to be the family fun police or a killjoy, so I kept my apprehension to myself.

The property hadn't changed a bit in nearly thirty years. Everything in the house reminded me of my childhood. It was like being transported right back to the 80s and yes, I loved it. Our daughter ran around the place like a mad thing. She was so happy to be there and to spend time with her grandparents. She wanted to stay in the same bedroom that I had slept in. Opening the door to the room, I'd swear it was the exact old bedspread.

That first night I was unsettled, finding it hard to drift off or get comfortable. The fresh country air and long walk in the fields had worn us all out, but I was the only one tossing and turning. I kept having strange dreams. Not bad, but unnerving. I was here in the farmhouse, but I was my daughter's age. I was an only child, and I never brought a friend along with me, but in the dream, it seemed like I was playing with someone? I woke up in a cold sweat and the feeling of unease intensified.

"Did I ever make any friends whilst we stayed here?" I asked the next morning at breakfast. I needed a very big cup of tea. I was grateful mum was still happy to take on the alpha parental role, flourishing in being able to dote on both daughter and granddaughter. She poured the warm, brown nectar into a mug before cocking her head a moment and then shaking it.

"No, dear," she replied, "we never saw anyone else whilst we were here. That was part of the appeal. You didn't appear to be lonely though. You spent a lot of your time in the garden playing games and entertaining yourself. You always had a good imagination."

She beamed with pride. Her imaginative daughter was now a barrister and topic of many of her Rotary meetings. Bustling about, she started buttering toast.

"Why'd you ask, love?"

Not wanting to admit to heebie-jeebies, I took a piece of toast and kissed her on the cheek.

"No reason," I called to appease her as I meandered back to the bedroom. Maybe that was it? My imagination. Yes, it did wander off sometimes and I had always been very creative as a kid. But it didn't feel like that was the exact explanation.

I tried not to let it bother me; it was an itch I seemed unable to scratch, and I just needed to leave it be. The family was relaxed, and it really was great to be away from the hustle and bustle of the police station and courtroom. My favourite pastime was watching our daughter unwind and go back to play-mode. Even at just seven, she would sometimes feel self-conscious talking to her dolls or making up games. Here, with no one else around and no YouTube or Netflix distractions, she spent hours in the back garden, having tea parties and playing hide and seek by herself.

"Just like you used to, dear," my mum had commented.

It was on the long drive home that the memories came flooding back. Due to the length of the journey, I was in the rear with our daughter while my husband was in the front listening to a rugby game on the radio. We were playing I-Spy, and then we began chatting about what the best parts of the holiday had been.

"I'll go first," I began. "I loved spending time with nanny and grandpa."

"I loved playing!" my daughter added with enthusiasm. "I will really miss being able to do that."

"Well, you can play at home, darling," I replied. "You don't have to be on the farm to have tea parties and make up games."

She looked right at me with those baby-blues, her lower lip stuck out just a touch.

"But I won't have Mr Tiggle at home."

You know that sensation when you're on a rollercoaster and it takes off super-fast and your stomach feels like it's dropped through the floor? Or when you hear some shocking news and you forget to breathe, just for a moment…

"What was that, sweetie?" I asked her, needing immediate clarification but wanting to play it smooth. Don't scare her now. Feign nonchalance.

"Mr Tiggle won't be at *our* home," she replied calmly. "He told me that he isn't allowed to leave the farm. He has to stay there so he can play with the next little girl who comes to visit."

I was ice cold yet sweat was pouring down my sides. In a flash, I remembered everything. My *secret* childhood friend who I only saw at the farm. He was the reason I loved to play in the garden and never felt lonely, because he was always there, keeping me company. But I wasn't allowed to tell anyone about him, or he would have to go away and take me with him. My *imaginary* friend who, to this day, I have *never* spoken about just in case...

Mr Tiggle.

He was a friend I invented over thirty years ago. No one in the whole world knew about him: not my parents, not even my husband. Hell, I hadn't even thought about him in decades. And Mr Tiggle? I mean, that was a pretty unusual name. So how the hell did my child find out?

"The thing is though, mummy," she whispered, "I'm not supposed to tell. Or he will have to go away and take me with him. So, don't let anyone else know, okay?"

Oh God...

The End.

Notes

This was an early piece that I wrote almost entirely for the intention of it being featured on Ghost Stories the Podcast. It was never meant to be particularly scary but does infer perhaps sinister undertones regarding Mr Tiggle and I liked the ambiguous ending here. Why had the narrator forgotten about him, and most importantly, what was going to happen now that her daughter had disobeyed instruction and spoke of him?

And for anyone wondering, yes, I really did kiss my Edward Furlong poster...

TRACK SEVEN

Jill - This offering is at the crux of it, a tale about obsessive love. About how far one would go for that perfect partner. I'll let you be the judge of whether you think this tale perhaps implies there was someone in her *life that she just couldn't wait to get her hands on ...*

Number 7 – Tainted Love.

HAVE you ever gotten that warm, fuzzy feeling when you first meet someone you really like? Your heart starts beating a little faster, you're beginning to sweat, and butterflies are swarming in your belly? That was what happened the very first time I saw Adam.

It was late November and very cold out. Oftentimes I'd walk home from work, but it had been a long, hard day and my feet were sore. I could spare a couple dollars to ride in the warm instead. Night buses tended to be pretty empty.

Sometimes a few kids heading back after a late-night study session, some shift workers maybe. Tonight, was much the same: a couple of nobodies here and there. I walked to the rear and settled myself in, welcoming the heat and the quiet.

The driver pulled over two stops from where I'd gotten on. That was when I saw him. Adam was a vision of perfection as he ascended the steps onto the bus. He wore a thick dark jacket, jeans that fit just right and a black beanie on his head. There was a backpack slung over one shoulder. He looked tired, scruffy and a bit worn down, but he exuded pure sex. After paying the driver he turned, and his fuck-me eyes met with mine for a second before he sat down. That was enough. That look was all I needed to confirm what I had already suspected. I was in love, and it was obvious that he felt the exact same way.

Destiny.

It was destiny.

Struggling to breathe, I stared at his profile. Drinking in every single detail, lust growing deeper by the second. He shifted in his seat a little and a soft moan escaped my lips without permission. Thank god there was no one next to me. Even the way he moved was so fucking attractive. When he reached his hand forward to push the bell indicating his stop, I could feel tears welling in my eyes.

No, Adam I wanted to shout, *my stop isn't yet, wait for me...*

But of course, I said nothing. I didn't want to alert the others to our secret. Experiencing a physical pain in my chest, I watched as he departed the bus. After thanking the driver, he began to walk off into the night. He looked up as he passed the window at the back, where I was sitting and staring at him, and he smiled. A perfect, sexy as hell smile.

That was it.

I knew, right there and then.
He had to be mine.

I COULD THINK of nothing else. I wrote everything down I could recall about him, not wanting to forget a single detail. I made sure to note the exact stops he had gotten on and off. I looked on Google Maps to see where the nearest houses were to the stop and tried to imagine which was his. I knew he must be at home thinking of me as well...god, he must be in so much pain. Was he frantically searching social media, seeking me too?

I dreamt of him that night, felt his warm body next to mine. It seemed so real that I cried actual fucking tears when I awoke in the morning and realised it was only a dream; that he wasn't there, waiting to greet me with his gorgeous eyes and sexy smile. Fuck! I wanted him so bad.

Work was torture. My concentration was shit. It was a good thing my customers don't expect too much conversation. I was lost, and he was all I could think about.

At last, it the end of the working day and time to get on the bus. I had stayed late again, making sure it was the exact same time as yesterday. I spent ages in the bathroom, ensuring my hair and makeup looked good. My heart was beating so damn fast as I stood waiting for the bus. I yearned to see him again. I felt as though my life depended on the moment he stepped onto the bus.

The driver pulled over and I got on. It was empty. Good.

I sat in the middle this time, so I could be closer to him. Looking out into the darkness, I clenched my thighs together. My breath came out in a little gasp, and I was glad

I was alone. If waiting for Adam to appear made me feel this good, just wait until he was inside me.

It was almost time...

What?

When he didn't get on at the same stop as yesterday, I felt a pain in my chest, as if someone had stabbed me. I was breathing heavy all right, but not from lust.

It's okay - I tried to reassure myself, allay the panic. Adam wants to get in some extra steps, that's why he is so freaking hot. He's getting on at the next stop instead. It's fine.

But again, there was no one. The physical pain was almost too much to bear this time. Why had he abandoned me? Where was he? Who was he with?

Argh!

Balling my hands into fists, I bit hard on my tongue to keep myself from screaming out loud in rage. I wasn't sure the bus driver would understand how betrayed I felt.

By the time I had left the bus and arrived home, I was boiling over with fury. How dare he forsake me? I would find him and make him pay! He had broken his promise!

No.

No, wait.

Not *him*.

It wasn't Adam's fault.

He was too perfect, I reasoned with myself. It wasn't his responsibility. He had been seduced, stolen away from me by some bitch! Some skeevy, nasty whore with diseases and filthy promises had taken him and he was helpless. He was probably with her right now, fucking her, but he would be thinking about *me*. Even when he came in her nasty hole, *my* face would be in his mind.

I forced myself to calm down and let my breathing

return to normal. My hands were bleeding where my nails had dug into my palms. See Adam, I will draw blood for you!

I took care to clean my wounds and then busied myself with my chores to keep from going mad. I was hungry, but not just for sex. I realised I hadn't eaten since meeting him,

(this yet again confirms How Deep Is My Love)

but the anger had resurfaced hunger pangs. My luck was in; there was enough food in the freezer to sate my appetite, but it wouldn't last for long. I needed to find Adam.

Sleep was pitiful that night. Nightmares of that whore, making him do stuff, dirty stuff. Seeing him beg and plead to be let go. He didn't want her. He wanted me! If I find her, I won't just kill her ... I'll make her suffer first.

Work was so fucking boring. I didn't have any new customers, and I was pretty much finished with the old ones. I tried something a bit different on one of them, but my boss didn't like it. Said the family wouldn't approve. I was only trying to make her look extra pretty for her big day.

Less work made it seem even longer for the end of the day to roll around. I made sure again to spend plenty of time in the bathroom. If my customer's family didn't approve, maybe Adam would? The lipstick was so dark it looked like old, stained blood. I was certain Adam would like it. I could see him staring at me as he boarded the bus, fantasizing about licking my lips, biting down on them, mixing the lipstick with my real blood...my god, I couldn't wait to see him. I squeezed my thighs again, instant wetness and arousal heightening every sense in my body. I knew he would be there tonight. He had to be.

And sure enough, he was. This time I was almost at the front of the bus. Again, there was no one else onboard. Just me and the driver. Then, the bus pulled over and fuck...as Adam stepped onto the bus, he looked straight at me. This time, our eyes locked. I let out an audible moan. This was it.

It took all of my power and concentration to stay seated. I had never felt like this. It would so be worth it in the end. I had known it would work. He came over and sat opposite me. And smiled. He had the most sensuous mouth I had ever seen. Perfect teeth. Heat rose over every inch of my body. I had to utilize every ounce of control I possessed not to grab hold of him right there. I could tell by the look in his eyes that he felt the same. Well shit, I knew the lipstick was a winner.

His usual stop came. He made no attempt to ring the bell. Again, I summoned up all of my emotions and focused on how much I wanted him, all the time looking right into his eyes, into his soul.

My stop next. I rang the bell and got up. Adam followed. As we left the bus together, he grabbed my hand. I couldn't look at him, didn't dare it to be true. But it was. We walked to my house. He followed me inside.

This was it. I closed the door and locked it. He was standing right next to me, so perfect I hardly dared to breathe. We took off our coats, dropped them to the floor and then...

He rushed forward, pushing me against the wall, and began to kiss me. It always started this way. I could see the lust in his eyes. Now that it was actually happening, that I had him, the thrill of the hunt was over. I could let him do all those things, but I'm too hungry. So, I let him kiss me, his lips moving from mine to my face, my neck. His blood was now flowing so fast I could smell it. I could feel his heart pounding.

He pulled off his sweater, revealing damn near perfect chest and abs. He was like a robot now, one thing on his mind. I kissed him back, gripping tighter and tighter. He was clearly into it, and as I wrapped my legs around him I could feel how much he wanted me. His cock was rock hard pushing into me and I almost caved. Afterall, I chose Adam for his looks. But it wasn't *that* particular hunger that needed instant satisfaction. Now that I knew his blood was at its fullest, I reached his neck with care...then bit.

Oh my god, he tasted even better than I thought he would. I sank my teeth in harder and deeper, literally guzzling his blood as it pumped out into my mouth in fast, hot bursts of deliciousness. I'm not sure he even noticed. The spell I'd cast over him was still in force. He was still trying to kiss me even though I'm covered in his sweet-tasting blood.

I pushed him to the floor and sat on him. He was moaning in ecstasy. In his mind this was all just some fucked up sex game, and he wanted me right then. Too bad he'd soon be too weak to do anything at all, let alone that. Tugging on his jeans, I pulled them low enough to release his throbbing cock, which was straining against his boxers. Then, in a slow and seductive manner, I removed my shirt and his eyes widened. I do a pretty good job covering the scars with clothing and make up, but with only a flimsy bra he could see where the hunters have tried to stake me. Tried and failed, I might add. Hmm. Hunters in particular always tasted delicious.

I looked at Adam. Despite having lost over half of the blood his body needed to survive, and being on the verge of passing out, he was still trying to touch me. He looked like he was close he might just come if I even touched his cock. Poor Adam. It'd all be over soon.

I bent down over him and ripped out his throat, draining every inch of blood from his body. As I looked down at him, laying very still now, I saw he was still utter perfection. The look on his face was sexy as hell. He hadn't even taken off his hat.

I'm always annoyed by how hard it can be to remove a human head from its body. They won't simply snap off; I have to work at it. And I couldn't rip it off to eat later like I usually do. No, Adam's head wouldn't be food. Sure, I'd enjoy the rest of him when I needed to. But his head was my final piece.

Once the head was in my hands, I stepped over dinner and walked over towards the locked cellar door. Not that I ever had guests, but in case someone broke in, you know, security. I turned the key and headed down the stairs to where the rest of him was waiting.

I was able to attach my trophy with ease. Although I've always excelled at ripping bodies apart, my job as a mortician has honed my skills at sewing pieces of them together. As soon as I saw him on the bus that day, I knew his was the head I needed to make 'Adam' complete.

There, my darling. Now you are perfect. You may be made up of several different people, but each part of you is exquisite. And all of you tasted amazing.

Life can be lonesome you see. Now that I have my Adam, I feel so much better.

Until the hunger starts again. But that's ok, Adam and I have decided we would like to start a family. The mortuary is just down the road from a very nice nursery...

The End.

Notes

The idea for this story germinated from something I read where the MC had created a relationship in her head and ended up killing the guy's wife so she could be with him. That idea of obsessional 'love' is scary enough in a thriller/real life type scenario but as usual I had watched too many episodes of *Supernatural*. This story was originally featured on the Tales to Terrify podcast back in January 2020 and sounded awesome read aloud. The version you read now has been altered slightly just to freshen it up but not too much. Maybe one day we will get to find out if she and Adam lasted and if they ever started that family she mentioned...

Those of you who have read more of my work may also realise I use the name Adam a lot. I even had to change a character in a different story in this collection as it was yet another Adam...Maybe Mr Nevill, or indeed Mr Cesare of *Clown in the Cornfield* fame, is more of an influence than I realised...However, I'd like to give special mention to Well Read Beard who thought Adam was in reference to the first man on earth.

TRACK EIGHT

*J**ill - As with many of her stories, this one could act as a warning. Against what I cannot tell you, lest it give away the entire ending. I can tell from the narrative that she enjoyed witing stories set in the 80's, relished the sense of nostalgia it evoked. Say hello to the night...*

Number 8 - Lost in the Shadows

MISSING – 10-year-old Timmy London last seen outside Main St 7/11 on 10/10/87.

Jason sighed and furrowed his brow as he looked at the latest poster pasted onto the window of the Blockbuster. Timmy was the third kid to go missing in Crystal River in as many weeks.

No one had seen hide nor hair of him since he upped and vanished after buying a Big Gulp at the store ten days ago.

Jason placed the rental of *Re-Animator* on the backseat and drove out to the drive-in where he worked the projector. That evening they were showing John Carpenter's *Halloween*, and his boss was expecting the place to be packed out.

Luckily, they'd managed to score Hunter's Hamburgers Catering Company to step in and whip up some patties alongside the drive-in's usual hotdog and popcorn vendors. When that many hungry teens were in the audience, they needed all the grub they could get their hands on.

Parking up behind the big screen, Jason was surprised but pleased to see Jenny London heading into the staff 'hut' they used for breaks. Jenny was one of their best servers; she could always be relied upon to hustle the dollars out of the patrons' sweaty hands. This was the first time she'd been back since her kid brother, Timmy, had disappeared.

Before he could pluck up the balls to ask how she was, Hunter of the Hamburger fame came running over to him, arms waving.

"Hey, youse, Chuck says I can borrow ya for a few. Capiche?"

Oh boy.

All thoughts of Jenny were forgotten as Jason looked over at the pounds and pounds of ground hamburger and onions waiting to be rolled into patties, flipped and fried.

You've gotta be kidding me.

Yet, despite being much more of a pizza than a burger kinda guy, Jason salivated at the delicious aroma being produced from the fryer in the truck. Hunter allegedly had some sort of 'secret family recipe', like he was the colonel or something.

"Only the best meat from the best cattle in the Midwest,"

Hunter was telling him. "I drove down to the ranch myself to make sure those beasts are perfect. I gotta rep to protect."

Rolling his eyes, Jason was mightily relieved when Shonie appeared to take over, allowing him to hot-foot it over to the projection booth.

He saw the film reels were ready to go, so he dashed over to the drinks kiosk to grab a coke. Once the movie started the servers would weave their way through the cars, taking orders and delivering dogs, but before the lights dimmed people got in line to buy root beer and popcorn from the vendors.

He was counting the change out in his hand while in line when he heard some high school girls behind him idly chatting.

"I heard from Sammy Campisi a vampire is taking them!"

"Shut up! It's not a damn vampire. Timmy was taken in the day; those dudes can only come out at night."

"Well, Chrissie Janz told me she saw that old guy with the funny eyes driving the ice-cream van right by Main Street just before Timmy got lifted."

Collective intakes of audible breath were drawn, and the girls all looked wide eyed and shaken.

"I knew he was a kiddie-fiddler," the redhead stated, arms folded across her ample chest.

"Large coke?"

Grabbing his order and nodding at the guy, Jack, behind the counter, Jason slowly wandered back through the crowd, picking up on other bits and pieces of idle chit-chat.

He noticed an older couple towards the back of the lot. The guy had his hands on his hips whilst the lady was waving her finger at him.

"I don't gets why we hadda bring the twins with us, we

coulda gotten a babysitter," complained the man, whilst the woman threw daggers at him.

"*You* mighta been happy leaving our babies at home while there's a serial killer on the loose, Glenn Chaney but I for one was not gonna do that!"

JASON MADE it back to his booth, but he had the unnerving feeling that something was amiss. He couldn't put his finger on it, and maybe it was just the fact it was already so dark during the fall evenings. There was a real chill in the air tonight, and not the usual carefree, fun-loving vibe that ran through the drive-in. Once the cooler weather and damp evenings arrived, spirits lowered, and this dreary atmosphere was magnified by the missing kids.

Suddenly Chuck came rushing over.

"Cut the feed," he ordered, "I gotta make an announcement on the PA."

This was unprecedented. For a fleeting moment, Jason wondered if there was a fire, or if someone had taken ill. But there were no alarms sounding, no car engines starting ready to speed off to the ER.

He did as instructed and there was a collective "what the hell?" and resounding "boo!" from the audience.

Resembling a rabbit caught in the headlights, Chuck began.

"Boils and ghouls, we interrupt this evening's viewing of *Halloween* on behalf of the Crystal River Sheriff's Department."

Genuinely unhappy, Chuck's voice hitched a little as he continued.

"I'm sorry to tell y'all that little Judith Cesare is missing.

Go home and check on your kids. Lock the doors. Thank you."

Feeling sickened, Jason brought the lights back on and heard the cries and sounds of doors slamming and engines revving. No one was complaining; they all wanted to get home and make sure their own families were okay. Panic had set in.

Heading over to the 'hut', Jason saw Jack from the drink kiosk. His shoulders were slumped, and he looked upset.

Remembering Jack lived next door to the Cesare's, he placed a hand on his shoulder.

"I'm really sorry, dude."

Sniffing, Jack took a bite of the huge, dripping burger in his hand.

"Thanks, man."

Jason watched Jack shuffling away and the smell of the burger hit his nostrils. His stomach growled. He hadn't eaten yet, not having found the time to grab a bite. He realised there'd be plenty left over at Hunter's truck now that the crowds were gone.

He noticed the New Yorker was chatting to Jenny, so he let himself into the truck. As he was heading to the grill, something yellow caught his eye.

A rain slicker. It looked much too small to be Hunter's.

Something told him to pick it up.

Looking at the collar, he saw a neatly printed name tag.

If lost, return to Crystal River Elementary school. Property of Judy Cesare.

What the-

All of a sudden, looking out of the truck, seeing his co-workers enjoying their burgers, Jason realised exactly what was happening to the missing kids…

The End.

Notes

I wrote this originally under the name *One Night at the Drive-in* for a Crystal Lake Publishing flash fiction contest. It got through to the voting stages but not the final three and that was just fine as I can share it with you now! You may notice a plethora of names you recognise with the two main characters of course being named after Jason Brant and Hunter Shea. It was yet another story that I just had a good time writing. Of course, it has a *Lost Boys* kind of feel to it with the missing kids so therefore the new title, *Lost in the Shadows* was a perfect fit.

And did you get the King reference towards the end?

TRACK NINE

Jill - The following story might make an excellent episode of Creepshow. There were a few lighter moments, but the majority of the narrative evoked a dark and sinister sensation. If I had to guess, I would imagine the author and narrator share a similar fear...

Number 9 - It's a Sin

WHAT IS YOUR GREATEST FEAR?

Demonic clowns maybe? The sound of breaking glass as an intruder enters your home? Your car crashing into a lake when you don't know how to swim?

What makes you want to run and hide under your duvet, like you're a little kid again?

For Sam, it was when something awful seemed, *real*... when he could imagine the thing happening to him. So many stories can be rationalized. That witch that lived in the old, abandoned shack at the end of the road, who cursed people and ate babies? She was nothing more than an old spinster who grew grumpy in old age and disliked nosey children. The vampire who lived in the neighbouring town, whose victims became frail and faded away, was just a hermit living in the time of consumption.

But what about ghosts? Not Dickensian-esque wailing ghouls with shackles and chains. Or angry poltergeists who throw things about and make young girls speak in weird old man voices.

Actual ghosts.

Oh, the reason that they scared Sam so much?

He had seen one...

WHEN SAM WAS YOUNG, he lived in a rambling old cottage, right in the middle of the countryside. The cottage itself was picture perfect, as was most of the village. His dad was the local policeman, and his mum was headteacher at the tiny primary school. The school was so small there were two year-groups in each classroom. Everyone knew everyone in Moreville, and it was just a pleasant, if a tad boring, place to live.

When Sam was ten, a new boy started at the school. This was almost unheard of. No one ever left the village; therefore, no one new could move in, let alone a ten-year-old boy appearing all of a sudden in the school.

But he did. Turned out there had once been a bit of a scandal in his sleepy hometown. There was a man who had been at university eleven years beforehand. He had met a girl and begun a relationship. Falling pregnant, but not telling the father, she had returned home to her parents and had the baby. The boy's father had tried to contact her a few times, but eventually presumed their affair was over. He carried on with his life, graduating and returning to the village. He'd never heard from her or her family again.

Until now.

It appeared that the man's name had been on the boy's birth certificate. Following a tragic accident, in which the mother and the grandparents had died, Social Services tracked down the father. Although he was in an obvious state of shock, he had done what was expected and had taken his son in.

Sam warmed to the new boy, Jack, straight away.

His skin was darker than most people in the village, and it was accentuated by his jet-black hair and soulful eyes. The village wasn't used to people who weren't Caucasian, and this made him very appealing and mysterious.

Everyone wanted to be his friend.

At the start, he appeared quiet, keeping to himself. Since the students were children, they were not privy to the full details of Jack's life prior to arriving in Moreville; just that after his mother had died, he'd come to live with his father. This was simply accepted with childish naivety, and it never occurred to Sam to ask any more questions. Jack was there and Sam liked him. That was it.

They did all the stuff normal ten-year-old boys get up to.

Rode bikes for miles. Made dens in the woods. Unsuccessfully tried to build a treehouse.

Fished for minnow, but only found newts. Used jumpers for goalposts in the park to play football for hours.

Jack never came over for tea, as Sam's mum didn't allow

pupils in the house – she said it would be inappropriate. And Sam did not get invited to Jack's; his dad was still getting used to one ten-year-old boy, let alone two playing WWF or pretending to be Hero Turtles.

After school finished each day, Sam would race back and grab some crisps and squash. Then, hopping on his BMX, he'd peddle as fast as possible to Jack's house and wait outside in the lane until he arrived, usually just a few moments later.

"Park?"

"Nah, forgot the footy and I heard Marty and his crew were going up there."

"Ponds?"

"Nope, Mum'll kill me if I get these trousers dirty again!"

"Woods then?"

"Yes!"

So off they sped, pockets bulging with sweets and a bottle of Panda Pop, channelling the kids from *The Goonies* or *Stand by Me*.

Jack came alive in those woods. No longer was he the shy, quiet, withdrawn boy from school. It was as if he could be himself when it was just the two of them.

Knocking about in the woods, they would spend hours making up stories to try to spook each other.

One of these tales scared the crap out of Sam, although he would never admit it.

It was a classic ghost-retribution type of fable, but the way he told it really increased the fear factor. It was as if it made *Jack* come to life. Like Pinocchio becoming a real boy.

The story was about a lad who was mistreated by his wicked family and eventually murdered. Then, he had come back to haunt them and killed each one off in a nasty and revengeful manner.

As this particular story was Jack's favourite, he would tell it over and over. He never had to think about it, the words just rolled off his tongue the more he repeated it. Sometimes he would embellish certain moments, making each death more gruesome. He relished in this, as if somehow he was reliving a scene from a film.

"He couldn't take getting the shit beat out of him no more. He knew he needed to do summat to get his mam back. So, one night when it was dark, he slipped into his mam's bedroom and slit her throat ear to ear then stood back as fountains of blood shot from her like water out of a hosepipe. Haha, yeah!"

Sam thought he'd seen too many video nasties. It sounded like something from *Nightmare on Elm Street* or *Friday the 13th*. Not that he had ever been allowed to watch that kind of thing, but some of the kids in school had teenage siblings. The boys would beg them to share such stories at break times.

Despite being one of the youngest in the Year 6 half of the class, Jack was smart and by far one of the most able students. Bright and confident in his work.

Which made what later happened seem even harder to believe.

You see, just a few months after he suddenly arrived in their lives, Jack vanished.

At first, it was presumed that he had run away. Tried to go 'home' - back to where he had lived before. As the local bobby, Sam's dad led all the initial enquiries. There wasn't any major concern at this point - they just wanted to find the boy and bring him back to the village.

But there was no trace of him in his former town. Nothing. Dad liaised with the local detectives, and numerous checks of his old house, school and friends were made, but no one had seen or heard from Jack since he had left.

Searching the trains and buses proved fruitless, as none of the conductors, drivers or passengers recalled seeing him.

Now it's important to remember this was a ten-year-old boy, in the late 1980's. He didn't have a mobile phone. There wasn't email, Snapchat or WhatsApp. He hadn't left a note to say where he was going, and no one had seen him leave. It was late November in Northern England and very, very cold.

As people in the community began to worry, extra officers were shipped in from neighbouring villages and towns. They came to speak to the children at the school.

"When did you last see him? Did he ever mention running away? Had he told you any secrets? Was he unhappy? Do you know of *anywhere* he might try to go?"

None of the pupils had a clue. As far as the father knew, he didn't have access to any cash. If he had somehow travelled out of the village, it was most likely by hitchhiking.

'MISSING BOY' posters went up. Appeals were made on the radio and TV. Important looking men in suits arrived and asked more questions.

Police searched houses, sheds and barns. Rivers and streams were drained, and woodland combed to no avail.

Without a trace, Jack seemed to have just...disappeared.

Gone.

When that sort of thing happens, especially in a tiny God-fearing area, people get very afraid. Not believing they could be harbouring a child killer; the townspeople assumed a stranger must have come to the village. Doors were now locked, and children weren't allowed to play outside on their own. Everyone was terrified that it would happen again...

But it didn't.

This seemed highly suspicious to some. Maybe they had too much time on their hands, or maybe quiet, mundane life starves the imagination.

The boy, who had seemed interesting and intriguing to the kids, apparently had a dark cloud surrounding him, according to the grown-ups. His past was shrouded in mystery. What *had* happened in that so-called 'tragic accident' that had killed three people? Again, without the internet, it was difficult to ascertain information. The accounts in the newspapers had been vague, providing no extra juicy details. Sam's dad tried to access the police files regarding the incident but found to his frustration that they had been 'mislaid'.

And with that, it seemed like they might never learn the truth.

The boy's father claimed ignorance. There had been a brief conversation with the social worker, who was overworked and underpaid and just glad to be able to find a suitable home for the child.

Sam's mother, as headteacher, tried to contact Jack's old school to see if there was any pertinent paperwork. But again, she was thwarted. In an age where files were handwritten, it was claimed the requisite information had already been sent. It must have been lost in the post. No, they had not felt the need to keep any copies and could not remember anything remarkable about the child.

Therefore, with no further leads, the enquiries began to slow down. Sam's new friend was by no means forgotten, and the missing posters remained on lampposts. Life, well, just moved on.

Except for Sam. He could not shake the idea that someone out there must know something. A human being doesn't just vanish into thin air. Jack was smart; he would not have run away in the middle of the night in winter without any money. He hadn't taken anything with him. The only thing missing from his room were his PJs, which he was supposedly wearing. He would not have lasted long in the freezing cold with just thin pyjamas and no shoes. The local area had been thoroughly searched, and there'd been no sign of footprints or anything that looked like there had been a struggle.

So, what the hell *had* happened?

NOT LONG AFTER JACK DISAPPEARED, Sam began to have The Dreams.

He often woke, thinking they were real, and every night they were the same.

Jack was nearby. But trapped. Despite hearing the call for help, Sam couldn't reach him. The surroundings appeared familiar, but he was unable to place them. Then Jack seemed to fall backwards. Sam would try to grab his hand but was too late. His fingers would brush Jack's cold ones as he fell into an abyss. His face fixed in a frozen scream, he'd point at Sam, calling, "You know..." Then Sam would wake, drenched in cold sweat.

Back then there weren't designated school counsellors or other people kids could talk to about stuff like that. Not wanting to share 'feelings and stuff' with his mates, Sam kept the night terrors to himself.

Maybe, if he'd spoken up, it would not have been too late. Perhaps then, *he* wouldn't have been the one to find Jack.

ONE MONTH after Jack had disappeared, Sam noticed an unusual smell in the house. Being an old cottage in a rural village, his home had a big open fire in the lounge and some antiquated excuse for radiators upstairs. That particular day his father was at the police station and mother had a staff meeting. It was the start of the school holidays, and he had moaned and groaned enough that they had agreed to let him stay home alone. However, he was to be locked in the house and was only permitted to call if there was any sort of trouble. Since it was the week before Christmas, reading and Legos were the only things on the agenda.

It was freezing in his bedroom, so Sam came downstairs instead, walking into the lounge with his book. He sat next to the hearth, hoping that being close to the fire would warm him up, but he remained chilled to the bone. Despite the flames crackling, he could see his breath. There was an old storage cupboard near the stairs with coats and boots and other assorted junk. He walked towards it, intending to grab a blanket to stop the shivers, when his nose twitched.

"What is that horrendous smell?"

Thinking maybe the cupboard was damp, or one of the wellies had 'something' on it, he opened the door. But it didn't smell like dog poo – it was more like...rotting meat.

There were plenty of farms around the village, and one day whilst out walking, the boys had come across a sheep that had been mauled by a fox. The body had been there for a few days during the hot summer, and Sam remembered heaving and gagging over the rancid smell and the sight of maggots and flies. Why on earth was that horrendous stench of rotten, gone-off flesh in his house?

Then, out of nowhere, he heard a noise.

Such as like he had never heard before and hoped to God he never would again.

"Gah-shh."

It was a raspy gasp, like a very heavy smoker might make if he had a nasty chest infection. And it seemed to be coming from right behind him.

At the exact same time, although it was already glacial, the temperature plummeted further, as if he were outside in the snow and ice. His heart was racing, and he couldn't imagine what had made the raspy noise or why the room had turned so cold. He was too scared to form any sort of rational thought. Rooted to the spot, Sam willed himself to turn around.

Then, the noise repeated. But this time it was accompanied by a blast of ice-cold air from just behind his shoulder.

Although petrified, he somehow managed to slowly turn around.

"Oh, God."

To this day it was difficult for Sam to explain exactly what he saw.

"J-Jack?"

His friend was right there. Only it wasn't quite...him. He didn't seem...*whole*.

Sam should have been ecstatic to see his missing mate, but he knew it wasn't 'him'. Not anymore anyway. Jack wasn't see-through, nor floating about expelling a trail of slimy ectoplasm. But he wasn't human.

Feeling sick to his stomach, Sam felt a warm trickle run down his leg. The absolute worst of it was Jack's throat and eyes. Although his skin had been a warm coffee colour in life it looked like old dishwater now, which made the bruises and swelling on his throat stand out even more. And his eyes, those dark cheeky eyes which were meant to have had all the girls running to him in a few years' time, well they were wider than could ever be natural, popping out from his head and streaked with red from busted blood vessels.

He turned and pointed to a door.

"Help-" he wheezed, although it came out sounding like Grandpa when he forgot to put his false teeth in.

The door Jack was pointing to went to the cellar. This area was off limits and a hundred percent Access Denied. It was never used. Despite 'No Go' areas attracting kids like a moth to a flame, being the child of a policeman and headteacher meant Sam did as he was told. His parents claimed it was unsafe and he had never, ever been down there. He'd been told there was mould and vermin, and it was dark with uneven flooring. The door remained locked.

Already at the height of terror, Sam felt there was nothing left to lose. What could a few red-eyed rats and black spores have over this bloodshot apparition? However, there was still the issue of the door being locked and no idea where his dad kept the key. Sam tried the knob, and, to his complete and utter surprise, the door creaked open...

"Urgh, oh, what?"

The smell was enough to knock him backwards. Looking about he noticed the boy was no longer present. Sam grabbed a torch from the coat cupboard, put one arm over his mouth and nose, and headed down the stairs. He descended with caution as each step threatened to give way and plunge him further into the unknown. He was absolutely petrified. Images of skeletal hands grabbing his ankles through the gaps in the flooring pushed him to the brink of insanity.

"Made it," he sighed in relief.

The torch must have been low on battery as it only omitted a lonesome pathetic beam of light. The bleak darkness gave him pause. If you can believe it, it was even colder down there. Antarctic cold.

Something brushed his forehead, causing him to call out in surprise, but it was just a cobweb. Still, his heart continued pounding.

Sam heard the guttural gasping noise again and knew 'he' had reappeared.

Part of him wanted to run screaming up the stairs. Yet, the crazy-curious side made him stay, intent on finding the cause of that rotten smell. Suspicions were well and good, but Sam needed to know, to be certain. Squinting, he could just make out a form by the far wall. Jack, or the thing that used to be him, seemed to be slumped over, looking down at the floor.

"Help."

Summoning every single last bit of courage and strength, Sam walked over to see what he was referring to.

Whatever he might have been expecting, nothing could have prepared him for that sight.

"No!" he whimpered, his hand flying up to his mouth.

A bony hand, maggots crawling up and over the fingers.

A dried scalp, part of which was undulating as a Deathwatch beetle emerged.

Sam's stomach revolted. Retching, he vomited, then fled back up the stairs as fast as possible.

Mind racing, eyes stinging with tears. He threw up again all over the hall carpet.

"Dad!"

His first instinct was to run to the police station and find his father.

Somehow Jack must have broken into their house and got trapped in the cellar. Crushed his own throat so that it looked like it had been flattened. That could happen, yeah – you could strangle yourself? Right? *Right?*

But something stopped Sam.

He remembered how his father had done 'all that he could', how it was now just a matter of waiting for new evidence. That he was positive the boy had run away.

Then he thought about how the police files from his old town had *mysteriously* been misplaced. How his own mother left him alone in the house, suggesting nothing else bad was going to happen in the village. The convenience of her files having been lost in the post...

Suddenly, as though Jack was somehow able to control Sam's mind like a TV remote, a scene from a past event formed in front of his eyes.

His father, reading a file, experiencing incredulity that a ten-year-old boy could cause such devastation.

"I read the goddamn file, Susan. This was no accident. That kid did something. They don't know what or how, but..."

"And look at this! The social worker has stated she had 'deep concerns.' There's something not right about this kid, Suze..."

Next scene: his mother tearing open a thick envelope from Jack's previous school, full of worrying stories about inappropriate behaviour and horrific pictures the boy had drawn.

"Kevin, you know that stuff from the police file? Take a look at this. His teacher has said Jack is a clever and competent child with a disturbing imagination. There are records of playground skirmishes, and oh dear god! Look at this picture he drew? We cannot let this friendship develop, dear..."

Next, his parents looking at each other, anxiety etched on their faces whilst watching the boys playing WWF in the back garden, their friendship growing.

Like a movie projected onto the wall, Sam now witnessed the night his friend went missing. He saw his father, sneaking into the boy's house. Jack waking, but not being frightened at seeing a policeman. His father placing a hand over his mouth.

The boy, unconscious, being carried into Sam's house.

Susan opening the cellar door...

Carrying him down, laying him in the far corner.

Sam continued to watch, the dread and horror growing in his stomach.

Now, his father was pressing his hands around the boy's throat whilst he gasped and gagged.

Jack's eyes grew more and more bloodshot as each breath left his body.

"Mum? No, mummy!"

Pouring quicklime over the body...

Then, decomposition beginning, the process being sped up by the chemicals.

"Oh, god." Bile rose in his throat as Sam saw the rats gorging on the gelatinous remains.

That dreadful smell masked, until now, by the cold...

And that was when it hit him.

Why Jack had come back.

And his intention.

See, he *had* been a troubled child. But it hadn't been *his* fault. His mother had despised and resented him. He'd been subjected to horrific abuse at her hands. And his grandparents? They stood by and did nothing. The horrific pictures he'd drawn? Depictions of what *she* did to him. Inappropriate stories? No, recounts of what she had done, Jack wishing to escape her evil.

Did *he* cause the accident? Yes. Because it was the only way to be rid of them forever...

Was he planning to repeat the cycle of abuse? Never. He wanted, *needed* a fresh start and was just beginning to settle into a 'normal' life. But Sam's parents were terrified of what Jack *might* do. So, they took matters into their own hands.

And now, unfortunately for Sam, Jack was going to make them pay in the only way he could and knew how.

An eye for an eye.

Feeling compelled, Sam walked over to the open cellar door.

Felt a sharp shove from behind.

Enough to send him flying face-first down those winding brittle steps, one finally giving way and crumbling beneath his feet.

He landed awkwardly at the bottom with a broken neck.

AN HOUR OR SO LATER, Sam's parents found him: head twisted the wrong way, a frozen look of fear forever on his face.

So, the reason ghosts scare him so much? Why he knows for certain that they're real?

Well ...

He is one.

And now Jack has a playmate forever...

The End.

Notes

This is the first story I wrote after I decided to jump back into it after many years of non-fiction work. The original version, just called *Boy*, was featured on Ghost Stories the Podcast, written in first person POV. I owe thanks to Hunter

Shea and Brian Moreland for the adaptation you have just read as they both helped me greatly to tidy it up, flesh it out and make it third person instead.

Because it is one of my older but well-loved stories, it holds a very special place in my heart. Two of my favourite names again which come up time and time again. I suspect Sam is partly an homage to the taller Winchester and although I often use Jack, I'll attribute this to Mr Campisi. Go Sox.

And I will never forget one of the mums on the school run once said to me, "OMG that was amazing. You're so talented but fuck me was I scared."

Result.

TRACK TEN

Jill – Another of her shorter works, one of those flash pieces that drops you straight into the action and leaves you wishing for more. There are several of this length I have discovered, but not many of this subject matter. They hit you like a sucker punch to the gut, and I suspect that was the sensation she was hoping for.

The plot may be familiar to some, but I applaud her bravery on that finale.

Number 10 - Love is a Battlefield.

As she passed through unfamiliar territory, the shaking began to worsen. Cold beads of sweat pooled in the dip of her lower back. Having read *The Running Man*, Heather knew this couldn't end well.

She was sure as hell no Katniss. There'd been no training, she had no street smarts. She'd never had to fight for anything. In fact, for her entire existence

(until now)

everything had been handed to her on a plate.

Weeping, she looked out of the window of the speeding vehicle. She didn't have a clue where they were heading. No one had told her anything.

They probably thought she was too fucking dumb to comprehend.

Passing the sights at an alarming speed revealed nothing. Of course, most of the land looked the same now anyway.

Heather wished for someone to talk to. To ask why, of all the survivors in her area, she had been selected. In the rush and confusion, her parents had been unable to explain. One moment she was there, albeit living in a perpetual state of fear, the next – gone.

Ever since the Rebellion had taken over, the wealthy had been made to pay, figuratively and literally. Those who had led a golden life, born with a silver spoon in their mouth, were now pariahs. *They* were the scum, the underclass. The Rebellion rose from their ashes like the proverbial phoenix, seizing control of the country. Storming the gated communities and country mansions. Killing many outright. Those left alive

(what a fucking joke)

had been evicted from their estates by force, whilst the forgotten classes moved in. Stately homes, ancestral manors: they all now belonged to the once underprivileged.

New laws and rules came to pass. Anyone who tried to stand up to them was executed. They declared it was *their* time to live like kings. No more welfare, no benefits handed out to those who had lost their riches. Now, *they* lived in cardboard boxes under bridges and begged for spare change. Lords, Baronesses, the nouveau-riche. None had been spared.

Then there was The Game. Heather presumed someone within the Rebellion worshipped Richard Bachman. Which was ironic, as he was likely now lying in a puddle of piss in an alleyway somewhere...

But unlike those stories, set far away in the future, this was happening right now. And what was behind door number four, the actual prize up for grabs?

Her life.

If Heather was able to get through The Game, which was said to resemble something from *Saw*, she would be given a Free Pass to live amongst the Rebellion. That was it. No cash prize, no dream holiday. Just her life.

Of course, the fallen rich had no real idea what The Game entailed. They were not permitted access to TV or radio. There were no phones or internet browsers for them. Their sole knowledge of the whole debacle came via word of mouth and rumours. Once a month, a member of the Old Ruling Class was selected to 'play'. It could be anyone. You could not volunteer, nor could a champion take your place. If you refused, you would be executed along with every single member of your family and community. The barbaric, fatal punishment had been sanctioned once so far. The image of seventeen innocents hung, drawn and quartered was burned onto Heather's retinas. Never would she forget the sounds and the smells that day. Ripping, tearing, choking, gurgling and wetness. Even worse, the cheers and laughter from the executioners.

And so, Heather had been chosen. She stood tall
(despite her inner turmoil)

when the guarded and armed announcer called her name. She took one last look at her ailing parents, bowed her head and, without a word, left to do her duty.

THE VEHICLE BEGAN TO SLOW. They appeared to have reached their destination.

After wiping the foggy window she'd made misty with her breath, she noticed what looked to be a deserted football stadium. The Rebellion despised any kind of celebrity status. Their decree ensured most of them had been *removed.* Those who earned millions kicking a ball around were some of the first to be disposed of. Thus, these multi-purpose all-weather stadiums were more or less desolate. Except, it would appear, when in use for The Game.

Flinging the car door open, her captors drug Heather out and through the entrance onto the pitch. Boggy and fetid dirt replaced the once pristine grass. Flies swarmed over large, dark patches, the smell not dissimilar to those seventeen rotting, disembowelled corpses. Stifling a scream, Heather tried in desperation not to disclose her terror. It would do her no good. She might have no idea what awaited her, but she was fucked if she'd give them the satisfaction.

Back home, in the compound, the rumours were abundant:

The Rebellion captured lions, paying homage to Roman times and making the chosen one fight to the death.

A glorified Fight Club, where the opponent wore spiked armour, and the defendant had no chance of surviving.

They bred mutants, created zombies.

Starved men to the brink of cannibalism.

No one knew for certain, but their nightmares were fuelled by endless possibilities.

Tormenting herself with impossible questions, Heather had played hundreds of nightmare-fuelled scenarios through her mind. She'd once been a fan of horror films, and the gratuitous torture scenes and vicious rape depicted in *I Spit on your Grave* now seemed all too plausible. And she was no Jennifer Hills.

It seemed just moments ago her name had been called, yet now it was time to discover the truth

(please, not cannibals)

 of what terrors she would face. Her lithe and unready body shivered in the cold as mist drifted across the grounds. Clinging to anything to help her cope, she pictured her father reading *Hound of the Baskervilles*, her head resting upon his lap as he stroked her hair. The only solace she could find was the hope her parents wouldn't suffer.

The Rebellion members marched her into the middle of the former pitch and then raced back to the sanctum of the covered pavilion as if scared for their lives. Heather looked in every direction, a million prospects running through her mind. Would they release some sort of monster now? Would she try to fight, or just let it maul and devour her? She felt warm liquid trickle down her leg.

Panic setting in, she thought, *why me? Just because daddy was a surgeon and made good money didn't mean we were bad people...*

She was rooted to the spot, quivering in fear. It seemed her bladder and perhaps bowels were the only parts of her capable of movement.

She was startled out of her stupor by an ominous sound to her left. Wide eyed, she spun in the direction of the noise.

It seemed oddly familiar, although the setting was all wrong, and how the fuck could they...

No!

Every single messed up scenario she had imagined now paled into insignificance. Nothing, *nothing*, could have prepared her for the reality.

She dropped to her knees, praying, begging.

"Oh please, please no!" she screamed. "I'll do anything. Please, not this, not –"

She didn't have the chance to finish her sentence. Stark realisation weighed heavy upon her. No prize existed. There had never even been a chance of winning and survival. Her death served purely as entertainment for the Rebellion.

Ripped apart and eaten alive, her final, dying thoughts were, *why? Why did th-*

Applauding another sacrificial feeding, the Rebellion cheered with gusto before returning to their pillaged homes. In one month, He would choose another.

Until then, they would celebrate...

The End.

Notes

This idea came from a Flame Tree Press newsletter contest. I believe the prompt was simply Dangerous Games and this King fan went straight to *The Running Man*. It isn't particularly original, but I like the finale. Which is ironic as I loathe open or ambiguous endings in books and movies myself.

That was until I read *The Box* by Jack Ketchum. Although we will never, ever know what was in it, that was the entire point. It drives people mad but also keeps them mulling it over. I'm not remotely suggesting *Love is a Battlefield* is akin to *The Box*, it is simply something that dawned on me as I was editing it for this collection.

TRACK ELEVEN

*J*ill - *Another recount amongst the papers, again told from the point of view of a teenager. I enjoy stories with differing timelines and that feel authentic. Of course, I don't know the author's past, but at least part of this 'legend' feels true. In fact, since we are in Somerset, I might head over to Trent Barrow and see for myself...just not on Halloween.*

Number 11 - Running with the Devil.

HAVE you ever had an experience that frightened you so much, you don't know whether you can ever bring yourself to discuss it?

That, somehow, to speak of it might make the event happen all over again?

That is how I *should* feel about the 'legend' of Trent Barrow.

Although, let me tell you this straight up – it sure as hell is not a fucking legend!

It all started many years ago, when I was just a kid. I lived with my parents in a small rural town in the county of Somerset. It was the eighties and life was pretty sweet. Get up, go to school, come home and play outside. In for tea, then back out until bedtime, where you slept like a log ready to do it all again tomorrow. Bliss.

My parents were pretty cool. I was brought up watching crime TV shows and reading horror. Our bookshelves were lined with Stephen King, M. R. James and Edgar Allen Poe. Listening to my dad tell ghost stories was the thing I loved the most.

For as long as I can remember, he would sit me on his knee and recount the various lore and legends of the local area. He had grown up in the neighbouring county, Dorset, and had many chilling and exciting stories to entrance me with. Some, I later realised, were tales borrowed from the classics – such as the *Tell-Tale Heart*.

But many others, he would swear to this day, were true. Things he had seen with his own eyes. And one particular tale, one he told over and over, could not possibly be fabricated.

This was the legend of Trent Barrow.

My dad told me that once a year, appropriately on All Hallows' Eve, a phantom coach and horses would manifest, racing through the barrow. Then, tragedy would strike, and the coach would plummet into the lake, disappearing until the next year. The legend said that the coach had been returning from a ball, when the horses were spooked and bolted towards the water. The entire party and horses disappeared into the bottomless pit and were never seen again...until the anniversary the following year, where the ghostly carriage returned to relive their catastrophic accident.

I would listen with chills running down my spine when dad told me that one year, when he was a teenager back in the sixties, he and a few of his mates decided to head down to the supposed location and see if they could witness anything.

Well, around 11:30pm, dad and another lad chickened out and headed home. But their other mate, a stubborn sort, said there was no way he was being a pussy. So, he stayed.

Dad and his mate went to see their friend the next day. There was no answer at his house, no sign of life inside. The phone just rang and rang.

Eventually, after four days, his mum answered the door. Looking upset and angry, she called to Derek. As he came down the stairs, my dad gasped in shock. Although Derek was only seventeen years old, and just four days ago had long, jet black greaser style hair, it was now brilliant white.

He never told them what he actually saw that night; all they ever knew was that he had been so frightened his hair had lost all of its pigmentation.

It blew my tiny mind.

Being my favourite story, I made my dad tell it over and over, especially as it neared Halloween each year. I never bored of it. I was fascinated with the idea of the carriage just…disappearing.

I created my own versions of the tale, injecting personalities into the victims inside the coach.

There was an elderly couple with their debutante beautiful-but-mute granddaughter and a mysterious, young bachelor who wore his cloak high covering his face. I may have been thinking of Highwaymen but that didn't matter. The coachmen were brothers, both supporting wives and many children, having taken over the family business from their father once he had passed.

I never forgot the legend.

As I grew, Halloween became more about parties and scary movie marathons than Trick or Treating and stories.

About dares and stupidity.

Scares and flirting.

And most importantly, a boy.

It's always about a boy, right?

It was 1996. I was sixteen, and in love. It's always love when you're that age. We were both in Year 11 at school, and I would have done anything for him.

Even attend a party on Halloween at his cousin's house, who lived a couple of towns over. Near Trent Barrow, in fact.

It dawned on me that this may well be a ruse to encourage an outing over to the site of the bottomless pit, and I asked him if there were any special plans for the evening.

Looking at me with those baby blues, he swore it would just be a bunch of kids from his cousin's school and his aunt would probably make us bob for apples or some shit. His older cousin would then drive us home.

I was torn. On one hand, a party with my beau sounded awesome and like something that would give me endless bragging rights at school. Also, he hadn't said a word about any night-time jollies. I didn't even know how close the house would be to the location.

But on the other hand, I *knew* that story was true. That those horses would be dragging a ghostly carriage to its doom. And I wasn't sure I could be *that* close without finding a way to witness it for myself...

THE DAY of the party arrived. Fortuitously, Halloween was on a Friday, so my parents had agreed and given me a very special 1:30am curfew. They trusted Aaron and had confirmed with his aunt that Luke's brother could drop us home.

I have no idea how I managed double maths, along with the other mundane lessons, when I was bubbling over with excitement.

As predicted, the other girls were mad with jealousy. Aaron was one of the most popular boys in the year, so I was already the object of envy. Attending a party with an older crowd in another town was the crème de la crème of coolness.

By the time I arrived home from school, nerves as well as excitement had begun to fester in my stomach. Although I adored Halloween, there was still the element of fright for me. It was after all, the night where the veil between worlds was at its thinnest, where ghosts and monsters were able to cross over. I felt a shiver of anticipation.

I didn't think Aaron's cousin and his friends would so much be into lore and legends as to watching *Friday the 13th* and *Nightmare on Elm Street* whilst drinking 20/20 and sneaking Lambert and Butler fags. I imagined the only scary thing would be ensuring any other girls attending kept their eyes off my man.

I just couldn't stop lamenting over how damn close we would be to Trent Barrow, and on the night where the phantom coach would pass through.

A car horn beeped.

"Bye, mum. I'll be home just after one-ish. Love you!"

I headed out to Aaron's dad's car, greeting him with a quick kiss as I slid into the back seat. He grinned, whispering in my ear, "I can't wait for this party, babe."

Arriving at the house, I wasn't surprised to see a ton of kids already gathered outside, and a lot of loud music being blasted through some speakers that had been rigged up in Luke's garden.

"Tell aunt Susan I want you guys home no later than 1:30am," Aaron's dad reminded him.

"Thanks, Mr Shea." I called, closing the car door behind me.

"Dude!" Luke walked over towards us, slapping Aaron on the shoulder and giving me a wink. "Grab a drink and have some fun, hey." He nudged Aaron, making smoochy kissing noises at us.

Laughing, Aaron turned to me, "Real mature, huh." He grinned, apologetically.

We held hands as he guided me towards the kitchen and grabbed a couple of beers. He brought me close for a long kiss, and I felt completely relaxed.

"Yo peeps! Everyone into the garden. It's scary story time...mwahaha."

Dragging me outside, Aaron plonked us down onto a rug on the grass and wrapped his arms around me. I was definitely feeling the love tonight.

The usual slumber party type stories were retold with various incarnations of *Bloody Mary* and *The Hookman*. I snuggled into Aaron, enjoying the atmosphere and feeling the buzz from the beer.

"J, why don't you tell that one about the horses?" Luke called over to me.

I wasn't the most confident orator, but I did my best, engaging the others in the tale of the disappearing travellers.

"And every Halloween, just before midnight, it is said if you are standing on the exact spot in the Trent Barrow woods, you too will witness the ghostly horses and coach disappear into the bottomless pit and hear their everlasting screams." Feeling that shiver run down my spine again as I finished my tale, I was surprised to see my audience captivated, staring at me, a mix of wonder and excitement etched on their faces.

"Trent Barrow woods are just down the road, ain't they?" asked Jamie.

"We should go and see the ghosties, wooh!" laughed Dean.

"You won't go, you pussy, you're way too chicken shit!"

What was happening? Did people actually want to go to the site of the accident and see for themselves if the apparition appeared?

"Well?" Aaron glanced down at me, "isn't this what you always wanted to do? You can tell your dad all about it."

My heart was pounding as I looked around. Jamie and Dean had been in the year above us and played football with Aaron. Jamie had turned seventeen a few months ago and had borrowed his mum's mini to drive over to the party. Dean looked like he'd been helping himself to the beers all evening.

I bit my lip. What was I waiting for?

"Come on, A!" Jamie called over. Aaron kissed my cheek and went over to his mate, whispering something in his ear.

Jamie slapped him on the back and announced, "To the mini!"

It felt wrong somehow, but my desire to at long last visit

the location of the phantom coach superseded common sense. I agreed to tag along, heart pounding.

It was, of course, pitch black outside, it being close to midnight in late October. Not knowing the exact rumoured location of the bottomless pit, we carefully wandered through the trees with torches until we found a stagnant pool of water.

This was it.

The moment I had been waiting for since I was a little girl, sitting on my dad's knee.

Looking at my watch, I shivered. 11:30pm. We were so close.

"Erm, Aaron?" murmured Dean, "I need to go for a piss. I'll, um, head back towards the car for a few, mate. Alright?"

I noticed Aaron smirk and wave his mate off.

Then there were three.

Jamie began pacing about, looking awkward. "You know what, mate? I'm going for a smoke. Back in 5."

Frowning, I watched Jamie amble away too.

Glancing at Aaron, I realised he didn't look too surprised. Was he expecting his mates to bottle it or...?

"Aaron?" I began, "what's going on?"

Turning, he pulled me close to him and pressed his lips to mine. We'd been together for a couple of months now, so this wasn't a surprise. He was always looking for a corner to sneak off for a snog.

Returning the kiss, I felt Aaron's hand creep up into my sweater. Again, not a shocker. He was always trying to cop a feel when he could. But this felt more – urgent. Pushing me up against a tree, he began kissing my neck, his hand snaking from my bra down to the waistband on my jeans. I could feel his hard-on pressing against my thigh.

Now, don't get me wrong. We were sixteen and had been going out for a while. I was pretty sure I loved him, and I was ready for what he was trying to instigate. But *not* up against the tree with his mates just around the corner, and certainly not when I was just about to witness the most important ghost-sighting of my life.

"Hang on there, lover." I responded to his urgency. "We are here to see a phantom carriage, the 'legend' my dad told me, remember?"

I somehow managed to twist my arm until I could see my watch again. 11:45pm.

Struggling now, I batted his hand away from the zipper on my jeans.

He was having none of it, his own jeans hanging around his knees now, the front of his boxers tented. He was still using his weight to push me against the bark, which was starting to hurt.

"Aaron!" I cried. "Back off, please!"

His breath was coming out hot and heavy, and he was making moaning noises; for the first time with him, I felt frightened.

Tears began to fall as I realised what might be about to happen.

Just as he began to fiddle with my belt, the temperature plummeted. It went from being a little chilly, to literally being able to see our breath fogging out in front of us.

"What the –"

The sudden freeze seemed to distract him, at least momentarily.

Taking my chance, I wriggled out of Aaron's grip and gave him a hard shove.

"Dick!" I yelled in his face. "What the actual fuck is wrong with you?"

I'm not exactly sure what sort of response I was expecting. An apology. Embarrassment. Even anger, his lust ruling over his usually sensitive mind.

What I did not envision was the look of pure terror etched on his face.

He was staring behind me, trousers still bunched around his knees. I noticed a wet patch forming on his boxers, but it wasn't from excitement. Aaron had pissed himself.

Trembling, I dared myself to turn around, to see what had caused such an extreme reaction.

Part of me knew what I'd see. It was after all, the very reason I was here.

The legend...

It came thundering towards us, clear as day.

Four beautiful, white horses pulling a Dickensian-looking carriage.

Two coachmen sat atop, guiding the animals. A rumble of conversation came from inside.

As it roared towards us, I could see a frown upon one of the coachmen. Then an attempt to steady the beasts, who were galloping too fast.

We heard a "woah there" and whinnying as the horses seemed to realise something was amiss.

Now, the look of pure panic upon both the driver's faces.

The frantic pulling of reins, then...

Neighing.

Screaming.

Crashing.

Splashing.

Banging.

And finally, silence.

The phantom had re-enacted its infamous journey right in front of our eyes.

And it was so much worse than I ever could have imagined...

Halloween night, 1899

The party at the Baron's country estate had been the usual frivolous affair, thanks to the young Baroness being a bit of a socialite, minus the scandal.

Still, there was only so much dancing and apple cider one could manage, and Lady Margaret Winstanley was glad to see the clock ticking towards midnight. Like Cinderella, she felt sure she would need to be tucked up in her four-poster bed by the time the bells tolled.

Feeling most grateful, she gladly stepped into the awaiting carriage that would take her back to her estate via Trent Barrow.

Davina Hamilton-Weston, a sixteen-year-old debutante, felt the exact opposite from the spinster Winstanley. She had enjoyed a glorious night of dancing. Her card had been marked by every eligible bachelor present, making her father, Lord Hamilton-Weston, most proud.

She had been glad of the carriage's arrival only as her feet were sure to be covered in blisters. The young debutante, however, was especially pleased to see one last person board the coach before its departure.

Rufus Brotherstone was a wealthy young bachelor and, it was alleged, a bit of a cad. That of course didn't stop Davina from stealing a glance at him under her lashes.

They had enjoyed a dance, and as he had led her breathless to the couch to rest after their jig, his hand had lingered a moment more than proper, causing her heart to flutter and cheeks to redden.

He smiled as he sat opposite her, and she felt her young bosom rising in anticipation.

The coach lurched as the horses began their journey, and she was jolted forward. Allowing gravity to give her a little push, she bumped knees with the gentleman.

"Davina!" her father reprimanded as she hurriedly scooted back into her proper seat, face burning.

Knocking on the roof with his cane, Lord Hamilton-Weston called out, "I say, chaps, do take it easy!"

"Sorry, Sir," came the easy reply from one of the coachmen, "mare got a bit spooked. Won't happen again."

"Hmph," muttered Lady Winstanley into her handkerchief, thoroughly disgruntled by the jolt and disgusted by the obvious devilry occurring before her very eyes.

It wasn't a long journey by coach back to their various estates, but the route would take them directly through the Barrow, which was apt to be a tad bumpy.

Davina wished that the horses would spook again, so that she might accidentally fall into the lap of the young man opposite her.

Oh, what a wicked thought. She ought to be punished for such brazenness...

Staring surreptitiously at the debutante before him, Rufus Brotherstone felt a stirring in his loins, thankful it was covered by his thick winter overcoat. She was devastatingly beautiful. He must find a way to win her over. Deflower her. Shifting in his seat, lest his intentions be known, he felt the coach judder again beneath him.

"Oh!" cried Lady Winstanley, as their comfortable transport began to rock a little.

Then, out of nowhere, came a yell from the coachmen, followed by a terrifying cacophony of noises from the horses.

"Woah there!"

"Daddy?" asked Davina, feeling frightened. "What –"

But she never got to finish her question.

As the storm raged and the horses grew wilder, a strong gust of wind blew one of the coach doors open and ripped it away, leaving a gaping void with no protection from the elements. The mere humans inside were no match for the velocity of the wheels and ferocity of the weather. Lady Margaret Winstanley was flung out with such vigour that she barely felt the spike from the fallen tree impale her like a lollipop. As the coach spun, Davina Hamilton-Weston too was tossed out like the winning caber and joined her fellow passenger on the ground. Alas, so great was the impact that it severed her spinal cord and she was decapitated. Her head kept on rolling until it reached the infamous pit.

Lord Hamilton-Weston had tried to be valiant and reach for his daughter as she flew into the abyss, but his own self-preservation kicked in and he grabbed a hold of the opposite door whilst wailing in anguish. Upon seeing the fate of his only child, he let go of his strong hold for a moment and was rewarded for his cowardice as the coach flipped and he too was evacuated from the interior in an unceremonious fashion. Screaming helped none, and his body landed in a nearby tree. It took around five minutes of pure agony for him to choke to death and succumb to the broken neck. He had been hanged by his own fancy collar.

The remaining passenger, Rufus Brotherstone, could only watch in terrified silence as the coach took its final spin and headed straight into the lake. The water began to seep into the carriage with ease since there was no barrier, and he tried in desperation to pull himself out. However, his arm had been wedged beneath the seating, which had been crushed in the fall, and he was trapped. By the time his lungs were filled, he was resigned to his watery death.

I STILL LOVE THIS STORY. Despite the scare it gave me, and Aaron turning out to be a complete bellend, it continues to give me joy. Apparently, I have told it so many times the nurses know it off by heart. No matter, they come and go so there is always a fresh pair of ears to bend. Afterall, they say I won't be able to leave this place…ever.

The End.

Notes

There is *some* truth to this story, though thankfully not the part about the tosspot boyfriend or ending up on a psych ward. But the actual legend of Trent Barrow in Dorset is 100% legit and my dad *did* tell me this one over and over as a child. It was the catalyst for my obsession/terror regarding the supernatural. This fascination/fear of all things ghosty has never left me and it is an unwritten rule in my house that we do not speak of spooks past bedtime. Yes, you read that correctly. This horror writer just admitted that she is fucking terrified of ghosts…

Well, they do say write what you know and write what scares you so…

TRACK TWELVE

Jill – the following took me back a little. It certainly made me flush although it was presented in such a comical fashion that I was able to giggle, even at the language and subject matter. Having two younger brothers, I could certainly attest to the likelihood of this scenario.

I feel that there is only one moral, one warning to adhere to – be careful where you stick it. And on that note –

Number 12 – Paradise City

"And who is this kid?"

"I've already told you. I've never seen him before, but he was coming out of Moyce's top set maths, and I was headed back to Barrett's class after I'd been for a slash."

"What form is he in?"

"I dunno, but I thought I heard Ross Jones say he was in Webbo's class."

"Tell me again what happened, use his exact words."

"Urgh, I've been through this like twenty times. He said, and I quote, 'I know about the tree. I have something that is gonna make you cream like never before'."

Richie licked his lips, the front of his trousers already tenting in anticipation. He'd made Tom repeat what the new kid had told him over and over, each time getting closer to making good on the proposition before they got anywhere near the rendezvous.

"And what time are we 'sposed to meet him?"

Tom checked his watch and scrunched up his nose. His father had insisted on this fancy contraption with bloody Roman numerals when all he'd wanted was a Casio.

"8 o'clock, so we have half an hour."

Richie forced thoughts of his great-aunt Nelly into his mind and was soft again quicker than Derek Dursley eating a battered sausage. No way he could bike all the way to Fowlow Woods with a boner. Besides, if what this kid said was true, he'd be needing all of his strength.

"How does this bellend even know about the tree? I was told if I ever dobbed about it, I'd get ripped a new arsehole."

Tom shrugged his shoulders.

"Reckons he followed a couple of year 11s out there and once they'd pissed off, he looked in the tree."

Smirking he added, "There was a folded-up picture of Sam Fox, a nice trail of jizz right on her tits."

Great-aunt Nelly, Great-aunt Nelly!

"Let's just get to the tree," puffed Richie, trying desperately not to imagine beating one off to Sam. "And fast!"

Arriving a little before 8 o'clock, the boys were relieved not to have passed anyone on their way into the woods. There was always the chance of happening upon a dog walker, and they didn't want that to occur whilst *they* were 'walking the dog'. Thankfully the tree was far away into the deep, dark depths where most casual members of the public never strayed.

Throwing down his bike, Richie ran to the trunk and retrieved the scrap of paper torn from The Sun. His mum was always muttering about how belittling and degrading it was to still have Page 3 girls, but he hoped the feature would never go away. How else was a 15-year-old who had recently discovered the pleasures of the flesh meant to cope? Whilst some of the lads boasted in the changing rooms about how they'd had a blowie from Kirsty McCann, Richie knew that he and Tom didn't stand a chance, even with the school slapper.

But somehow, they had been allowed into the very exclusive Tree Trunk gang. Actually, it was no secret how they got in. Tom had an 18-year-old sister at the local tech college with tits almost as big as Miss Fox. All it had taken was one sneaky polaroid photo of her whilst she danced in her undies to 'Girls Just Wanna Have Fun', and they were sorted. Tom had felt sick at first knowing the year 11s were tossing off to pictures of his sister, but once he had tasted the delights the tree trunk had to offer, any residual guilt was out of his body faster than he could put it back into the hole.

You see, like Narnia or The Enchanted Forest, this tree was also magical. It even transported you to another world for a couple of minutes (if you were lucky). They didn't know and couldn't give a crap who had discovered it. They just knew they never wanted to be without it. An ancient Oak with a thick trunk, it somehow knew exactly what was needed. On one side of the base was a larger hole, high enough to not be noticed by a pesky passer-by and deep enough to store treasure. Namely bits of newspaper and, if they were really lucky, an old, crumpled and sticky but still perfectly usable copy of Playboy. There was occasionally the odd packet of fags or a beer can, but Tom and Richie weren't bothered with them.

And those wonderful centrefolds weren't even the main prize. That was on the opposite side where there was another hole, this one much smaller. Just the right size and height for a dick. Having yet to experience any kind of sex except with their own pumping fists, the sensation and reward for sticking your nob in a tree was mind-blowing and load-blowing, literally. But before either one of them could take their blessed turn with the hole, there was the issue of the new kid and his promise of the amber nectar of orgasms.

"Well, he ain't put nothing in here. I've used this picture at least three times already." Richie's hand was on the front of his trousers, rubbing his cock as he looked at the well-used clipping. That tosser better get there soon or he'd be in that tree like a rat up a drainpipe; he couldn't be expected to hold out much longer when he knew what was waiting for him.

In truth, the boys had become more than a little obsessed with the lure of the woods and the pleasure it gave them. Neither would admit to it, but both even dreamt about that hole; the thought of coming to (and cumming in) the tree more alluring than any girl they could picture, even Miss Fox. And yet they would often wake covered in cold sweat rather than the usual kind of wet dream. Alongside the temptation of fulfilled desire there was almost a sense of foreboding. Like a jealous lover, there was an unwritten rule they must never stray. Still, it beat wanking into a sock that was for sure, even with the unspoken malevolent threat.

"Calm down, mate, it's only just –"

Tom stopped mid-sentence upon hearing crunching through the leaves behind them. The boys were used to coming into the woods in the dark and always brought their torches. Richie even had some ridiculous helmet with a light on the front. He claimed it had been his granddad's when he'd worked down the pits. Tom wasn't sure what granddad Brant might think of its latest incarnation – allowing his grandson to have the use of both hands...

As the new kid stepped into the beam from their torches, the sun seeming to have packed up and done one in record time, he had a strange expression upon his face. It was usual and even expected to feel a little embarrassed, unsure and maybe a tad afraid upon your first visit to the tree. Despite handing over the pseudo-pornographic photo of Tom's sister as clout, Richie had still been nervous on their inaugural trip to toss-town. Part of him, the part that had been bullied without relent at primary school, had expected one of the older boys to take a photo of him with his wang out, fucking the tree. They'd blow it up, photocopy it and stick it all over school, especially in the girl's bogs. He could just imagine Kirsty the slapper laughing at it whilst she took a piss.

But this kid didn't look apprehensive or sheepish at all. In fact, it was hard to read him, his face seeming to lack any sort of emotion at all.

Richie decided to man-up; sometimes his need not to be ridiculed again took over, and a nasty, defensive side crept out.

"Well, you got summat for us or what? 'Cause if you've just come to look at our dicks, you can fuck off again."

Tom cringed. He was used to Richie's sometimes spiteful tongue, but he didn't know the temperament of this kid. There hadn't been time to discover anymore about him, and as per usual, the boys' common sense had been overruled by the power of their nobs.

The boy didn't acknowledge Richie's jibe. Tom noticed his eyelids looked heavy, as if the kid had trouble sleeping. His appearance and demeanour suddenly seemed much older than at school. Come to think of it, what form did he say he was in again?

But before Tom could clarify, the boy spoke.

"It's already done. I left it in the hole."

Spitting on the floor like some old cowpoke ridding himself of tobacco, Richie answered with a dismissive and condescending tone.

"Fucking liar, there ain't nothin' in there 'sides a well old Sam Fox picture, and I've already used that loads. Cum so hard the next kid had to wait for it to rain to clean the hole out again."

Great, so he'd moved on from being rude to boasting. What could be next?

Again, the boy looked neither impressed nor perturbed. He nodded to the other side of the tree, where Tom was standing. Not the hole with the good stuff, the hole you gave stuff.

"Other one." He clarified.

And then, without waiting for a reaction, he sloped off into the woods from the direction he had emerged, which was opposite of the way back to the housing estate.

Odd.

"Maybe we should," Tom began, but for the second time, he didn't get to finish his sentence. Richie proved he would be a beast on the rugger field should the need ever take his fancy, and he almost sent Tom flying as he shoved him out of the way in eagerness to get to the hole. By the time Tom rubbed his shoulder and turned to say something, Richie already had his joggers and pants around his ankles and was jamming his dick into the hole.

It was funny how none of the boys ever considered that no matter their height, the hole was always just right for them. You never needed to be on tippy-toes or crouching. From the smallest year 10 (Tom) to the lankiest year 11 (Kevin Spearmen, who was around six foot already and had a 70's porn-star 'stash only his father could be proud of) the hole was always perfect. How could that be?

"Riche, I don't –"

But there was no third time lucky. Tom was yet again cut off, only this time it was by the screams emanating from the boy with his dick in the tree. You'd be forgiven for thinking for just a moment that maybe the screams were from the throes of passion. That at last, Richie really had found heaven in a hole in a tree. But no. This was not the sounds of ecstasy as one releases a hot torrent of cum into a welcoming void. This was pure and utter agony, and terror. And as Richie stumbled backwards away from the hole and ended up on his arse, Tom saw why. And he started screaming too.

Then instinct kicked in, and he tried in desperation to stem the blood flow from Richie's now dickless crotch. It seemed to be pouring out at a frankly alarming rate, and despite removing his shirt and wadding it against the wound, the fabric was soon sodden. Richie had stopped screaming, thank God; his eyes having rolled into the back of his head. He still wore the headlamp helmet which at least meant Tom was able to use both hands to try and work out how to stop a bleeding cock, or non-cock. He recalled something about keeping severed fingers as they could be sewn back on, so he left Richie for a moment to see if he could spot the amputated penis. He scanned the floor underneath the hole, looking around and praying he hadn't stepped on it. Ah, there was something there, something visceral and gore-covered and, oh shit on a brick – it was a ball. A bollock. Not being able to hold it anymore, Tom retched and puked all over the gonad. Somehow, Richie had been subjected to a full castration. He whimpered as he looked over at his friend. Richie was still unconscious, the fountain of blood where his nuts had been ripped off had now entirely soaked through the shirt and was staining the grass where he lay.

Still believing he could maybe help Richie; Tom shone his torch into the fun-spot. More bile rose into his mouth as he took in the sight of way too many bodily fluids inside such a small gap. Though there seemed to be blood and jizz aplenty, he couldn't see the missing member. Summoning every last inch of courage, he stuck his hand into the hole.

He wasn't sure how to respond to his discovery. As he brought his arm back out, the stump spurting blood faster than he could have imagined possible, he just stared at it. He honestly didn't know where the teeth had come from. He gazed at the amputation and his mind began to feel foggy. Realising what came next, Tom did the only thing he could think of. The thing that had been controlling them all along, ever since they were first introduced to the tree.

Tears streaming down his face, he accepted his fate and stuck his dick in the hole.

The End.

Notes

So, this story was entirely inspired by the novella *The Special* by James Newman and Mark Steensland. Theirs is way more detailed and a hell of a lot of fun. It's even been made into a movie which you can find on Prime. *The Special* is of course about addiction and how quickly it can spiral out of control and the depths you may sink too once you are fully under its control, no matter the vice. Teen boys with their hormones came straight to mind, and the power of a hole anywhere that could give you so much endless pleasure. They never even consider the origin of the tree, or how come the hold fits everyone? Hell, Tom and Richie don't really even question the motive of the New Kid, they just foresee more time in toss-town.

Richie is another nod to one of my favourite King characters.

TRACK THIRTEEN

Jill - The authenticity of the narrative suggests veracity, and if I am to believe the epilogue, well, it chilled me to the bone. One for sleepovers and school camping trips, perhaps? You decide.

Number 13 - School's out forever ...

LOOKING BACK, it was a fucking stupid idea. We could have been hurt, and we could have been caught. Either would have caused us a bucket load of trouble with our parents. But you think you're invincible when you're a teen, don't you? Immortal and untouchable.

Unless it all goes shit-shaped...

"ARE you sure we should do this?"

"Um, duh, of course we shouldn't! If we were allowed to go there, it wouldn't be cool."

The sun was high in the sky, its beams traipsing across the field and indicating we still had the whole day to play with. Despite the fact nothing bad ever happens in daylight, I felt a definite flutter in my tummy.

However, this was not the time for second thoughts. If we did this, we would have the best story to tell and would, at least for a day maybe, be the coolest kids in Year 9.

It was equal parts exhilarating and bloody terrifying.

I'd never done anything like this before. Ever since I was a little kid, I knew that I wanted to be a police officer when I left school, and I therefore had never partaken in any teenage high jinx.

Until now.

I found myself ambling across the fields behind my house with my best mate Lou. We were heading off on an adventure that, at the very least, involved possible breaking and entering (not to mention trespassing) and, at worst, could lead to one of us being injured.

You see, against all common sense we were heading to an old, abandoned building in the depths of the village, and we were going to find a way in and then brag about it.

That was the plan.

Now, I should also ensure you realise it was 1991. There was no such thing as Instagram or any form of social media, or even mobile phones that weren't the size of bricks and only used by bankers in the city. Kids would have to take our word for it as there was no way to document it, no concept yet of 'if you don't post about it, did it even happen?'.

You might be wondering: if we weren't obligated to provide photographic evidence, why the hell didn't we just lie? We could pretend that we'd been there when in truth we'd never left the house. Who the hell would know?

Well, there was this sense of honesty I guess back then; it never crossed my mind to fabricate a story.

So that was how we found ourselves arriving at the 'too inadequate to keep a bird out' fencing, which held a faded piece of wood stating 'No Trespassing' in sloppy handwriting.

This was the closest I had ever come to breaking the law. My hands were sweating, heart pounding, but I was fuelled by Lou stepping through the gap – she was always braver than I – and the thought of bragging about it to the well-fit Justin on Monday, and I followed her in.

You knew there'd be a boy involved, right?

"Shit, Lou. It looks well rank in there."

"Don't be such a pussy, we gotta go in now, ain't we?"

I was gutted to see that the years and weather had not been kind to the building. It was in a severe state of dilapidation, bordering on dangerous. I hoped the doors would be padlocked and the windows nailed shut.

The sign was still visible, nailed up on the side of the building in a place of pride.

THE BARWICK SCHOOL FOR BOYS

And because this place had become the dog's bollocks, mainly for a sneaky fag or snog or, like us, for the kudos it would bring in the common room, someone had graffitied the word 'Prison' over the word 'School'.

And I guess in a way that was correct. You see, before it was closed down in 'mysterious circumstances', this was indeed what my mum referred to as a school for 'naughty boys'. Kids who'd been expelled from mainstream education came here, and if they failed, next stop - a one-way ticket to Borstal.

It had an urban legend status. Stories told of people rocking up on Halloween with Ouija boards and shit so they could try and communicate with the boys who used to live here.

I wasn't too sure about stuff like that. I'd read a book called *Hell Board* and it sounded like a fucking bad idea.

Lou was grinning like the Cheshire Cat and already climbing through one of the broken windows. We'd been besties since we both found ourselves in top set English in Year 7. The teachers were always nagging at us that if we wanted to get our predicted A at GCSE, we needed to stop chatting so much. It had been her idea to come here once she'd found out about it from some of the Year 11's on the bus. Always the sucker for a chance to be a rebel.

Since I couldn't stay outside on my own without looking like a total bellend, I headed in after her.

"Shit!"

It was pretty dark inside, which shouldn't have been that surprising since they hadn't paid their electric bill in years. Or indeed, had working light bulbs.

It also smelt disgusting. Like a tramp had used it to take a shit and then invited all his tramp mates to take a shit too. It was nasty!

"Fuck's sake, J," called Lou, "get your skinny arse over here and look what I've found."

Gagging for dramatic effect, emphasising how much it stank and that I wasn't happy, I wandered over to see what she had discovered.

Books.

Loads of books.

Exercise books, reading books, library books and so on strewn everywhere. Those on the floor were muddied and ripped. They looked like they'd been nibbled on and used as nests by mice or rats…or worse.

There were also bits of paper still on some of the desks, so we must have been in one of the classrooms. One desk still held an exercise book and pencil, ready for the day's work. It was weird and unnerving, to the extreme. Fucked up, big-time massive.

Like the boys, and staff, had literally just upped and left. Or disappeared like that American place we'd learnt about in history, Roanoke was it?

"Come on," said Lou, ever the enabler. "Let's see what other shit we can find."

I must have looked reticent, and she was a sneaky cow, so she added, "You can tell Justin all about it at break-time tomorrow."

Damn those teenage hormones.

Off we went, further into the former living space of many 'naughty boys'. We walked through the rest of what looked to be classrooms, and I almost lost my shit when a couple of pigeons appeared out of nowhere, fluttering their wings.

"Jesus fucking Christ."

Lou was pissing herself when we turned a corner and the stench of damp and mildew and god only knows what else hit us. We'd reached the corridor where the staff offices had been. Now, it wouldn't take a genius to work out that it would be chilly in there, considering there hadn't been any form of heating for several years. And despite it being a warm day, it was still cold inside, likely due to it being dank and dark from the absence of light.

But honest to god, when we turned into that corridor it was like stepping into a freezer. I could feel goosebumps on my arms, and although it sounds cliché, we could see our breath as we walked down towards the door marked Head.

I don't know whether Lou couldn't feel it, or whether the stubborn cow was ignoring the warning signs. Turning back to me with her classic grin that always won me over, she whispered, "Jack pot!"

Yippee Ki Yay.

Fuck.

My heart was thumping in my chest so hard I was sure it would wake the dead. It seemed as keen to piss me off as Lou did. I kept thinking of those stories about the Ouija board and wondered if there had been some sort of presence trapped here and they'd released it?

Honest, my imagination was running wild and there was nothing I wanted less right at that moment than to open that door. Lou had a wicked gleam in her eyes as she stood in front of it. She'd been the one chatting with the Year 11's on the bus; I'd been too busy reminiscing about Justin asking to borrow my pen in French to listen to much of what they were bitching about.

"Do you know what Dale told me, 'specially about this old bastard?" she said, hitching her thumb at the door. "Apparently the reason they shut this place down was 'cause the teachers were paedo's. And this piece of shit used to beat and rape the boys as punishment."

You know when you start to get a really, really bad feeling about something? That there are certain things you shouldn't mess with, no matter how many bragging rights it gives you. 'Cause at the moment, I was thinking I would never get a snog with Justin if I was, well, dead.

"Lou?" I began, a tremble in my voice alerting her to my nerves. "I don't think we should go in there."

Of course, *she* was loving it. Not being easily scared,

she'd introduced me to the concept that sleepovers equal raiding your dad's VHS horror collection and watching as many Freddy or Jason films as possible.

I enjoyed all things spooky also, but with one big difference, I liked to be scared within the comfort of my own home where I knew what I was watching or reading wasn't real. King and Keene couldn't cause me harm when I had my duvet to protect me, even if I wouldn't allow my feet to peek out of the covers.

Coming face-to-face with a potential malevolent spirit had not been on the agenda.

The cow actually cackled in glee as she threw open the door.

And disappeared inside the dark room.

I stood there for what felt like hours before, against my better judgement, I followed. I hadn't heard any crashing or screaming, so unless I walked in and she was hanging from the ceiling, I was pretty sure she hadn't been murdered...

Yet.

"Boo!"

"Argh! You fucking bitch!"

I couldn't believe I'd fallen for the old 'hide behind the door and scream as you enter' trick, and there very nearly was a murder at that point. Or at the very least a pair of dirty knickers. Mine.

I punched her on the arm, scowling and willing my heart to return to a semblance of normality.

What remained of the office was sparse: a huge wooden desk, an old spinny-on-wheels chair behind it; on the far wall, an empty bookcase. It was odd, considering most of the other rooms looked as though school had literally been in session when they all just done one.

"There's something written on that wall, J."

Pointing towards the back of the room, she scrunched up her eyes to try to see clearer.

"What's it say?"

It was a useless blur to me but judging by the other amateur graffiti we'd seen sprayed around the place, it was possibly a tag.

There was still a blind on one of the windows, so I took care to step over the broken and dodgy looking floorboards to see if I could let some light in.

"God damn it!"

Well, I did manage to clear the window as the blind fell to pieces in my hand. "Ta-da! Daylight, your majesty."

Expecting some sort of witty retort, I was shocked for a moment to see Lou appear lost for words. And rather ill at ease.

Then I realised why.

The light from the window had indeed illuminated the room enough for us to be able to see what was written on the wall.

In large, dark reddish-brown letters were the words GET OUT.

It *could* have been spray paint. A very specific colour and with the ability to look like it was dripping, but it could have been...

Who was I kidding?

We were staring at a message, written on the wall of the office of the head, who was at the very least complicit in the abuse of these kids.

There was no denying it had been crafted in blood.

With a very specific instruction.

GET OUT.

"Lou," I began, "I think we should –"

Bang.

All of a sudden, the desk shot across the room as if being pulled by an invisible rope.

The chair was next; it came hurtling through the air towards us via an undetectable force.

That was it.

"Run! *Now!*" I shouted, pulling Lou out of the room.

We pegged it back through the building and I swear I could feel something following us. For once I was leading, and despite being shit at PE and always last on Sports Day, I was doing a bloody good job at motoring through the rooms. Wanting to get the fuck out of there was all the motivation I needed.

Then...

I heard Lou scream.

This time it wasn't the fake 'made you jump' noise, it was a real terrified *I've hurt myself* wail of anguish.

Spinning around, I saw she had fallen.

She'll swear to you, to this day, she was grabbed from behind.

Racing back, I clutched her hands and hauled her back upright, and then we scarpered.

I reckon we ran all the way to mine, never stopping to look back.

We burst into the kitchen, disturbing my mum who was having a cuppa and watching *Neighbours*.

"What on earth have you two been up to?" she demanded, and boy did I get a bollocking when we told her what we'd done. Once she checked Lou over and made sure her ankle was ok from her 'trip', she sat us down in the lounge, resplendent with frowny face so I knew I was in the shit.

"That place is not safe, girls," she scolded. "I think you are both very lucky to have just come out with a scare. I don't necessarily believe in all the mumbo jumbo, but there is something evil about that place for certain. One of the former masters is serving a life sentence for murder, and at least one of the poor boys killed himself right on the property."

Nausea threatened to sweep over me as this information sank in. It's one thing for a bunch of older kids on the school bus to tell you something, but when your mum confirms it and embellishes all the gory details, that is when the nightmare becomes reality.

"It was shut down after an investigation following the suicide. The authorities found a cellar, with ropes. Apparently, it was freezing down there, and the poor children were stripped naked and tied up as punishment. Left for hours. And", she added, her eyes filling with tears (mum is a proper softie), "there was evidence of sexual abuse too. No matter what those boys had done to be there in the first place, in no way did they deserve that."

Lou just looked down at her lap, and I began to realise the enormity and stupidity of what we'd done and how much worse it could have been.

"I'll put the kettle on."

Off mum went, wiping her nose, because everything is okay once you've had a cuppa, right?

Epilogue.

Years later I looked into the story of Barwick School for Boys. And it was all true.

There are lawsuits ongoing. Many of the ex-residents have suffered with life-long psychological damage from the torture they endured at the hands of the people meant to be there to look after them.

I'll never know *who* didn't leave; who still roams the corridors. Was it the spirit of the kid who hung himself, guarding the place against any further atrocities? Was it one of the former masters, come back to try to finish the job? Or something else, released by the Ouija board and attracted to a place that was literally oozing in evil?

I am pleased to report the place was torn down in the mid-2000's. So at least the building is gone.

But will that have ridded whatever lurked there, or are they just waiting to be rediscovered?

The End.

Notes

By now, you will be well acquainted with the fact I am wuss. The fact of the matter is, I am deathly afraid of the supernatural for a very good reason. I have witnessed my fair share of occurrences. The above story is true, albeit embellished. I suspect those of you who know me will get that this Lou is named for one of my BFFs, Ms Yardley.

That school did exist. I really did walk those abandoned halls and scare the crap out of myself. The poltergeist physical activity was added for dramatic effect, but everything else is legitimate. It oozed malevolence. I felt scared and dirty just being there. And when I came to look it up years later, I found out about the court cases. Allegedly, one of the old masters is holed up in Broadmoor on a murder charge. After reading several reports of sadistic sexual abuse that the police are investigating, I finally knew why I had felt so uncomfortable in the place.

It really was a school of evil.

TRACK FOURTEEN

*J*ill - *Some of the stories I have found, have been short but by no means sweet. It would appear anytime camping is mentioned, it is unlikely to end on a high. It could be why I stick to hotels. Or will this time be different?*

I'll let you decide...

Number 14 - Living on a Prayer.

PLACING a hand over his brother's mouth, Alex whispered, "Shh, Mikey!"

Something had woken them. The muffled noises emanating from their father's tent sounded ominous, and Alex felt vomit rise in his throat. Poor Mikey was close to pissing himself.

Whoever,

whatever,

was in there, was likely headed to them next. But Alex wanted to believe that if you were super quiet, the bad things went away.

Dad would be okay.

That's how it worked, right?

Right?

Poor Alex.

That *thing* was just getting started ...

"When you're sliding into third and you need a juicy turd, diarrhoea, diarrhoea ..."

Rolling his eyes at his ten-year-old brother, Alex was relieved to see Mikey relax and enjoy himself a little. It had been rough since their mother was murdered by an unknown intruder who broke into their home.

When they arrived at the lonesome campsite, Alex thought that this might be just what the three of them needed.

"Be nice to be off the grid for a few days," their father had told them.

Smiling, Alex thought of campfires sizzling with sausages and beans. Of fresh air and fireflies. And being away from their now tainted home.

They'd packed lightly, just the absolute necessities. This was a 'back-to-basics' trip, and their father wanted to rekindle some of his own childhood memories with his pop and Uncle Kevin.

"Please? I promise, if I have a nightmare I'll go over to dad. But can I stay with Alex?"

Despite suffering from night terrors since the break-in, Mikey wanted to sleep with his big brother. Alex didn't mind, so long as he could read some Jack Ketchum,. In fact, he'd prefer not to be alone.

They sat next to the crackling flames, drinking cocoa and looking at the stars, and things almost seemed okay with the world. Moving into their tents, Alex told Mikey he'd just be a minute whilst he drained the snake. As he relieved himself, he prayed his little brother would get through this trip and maybe, just maybe, the bad dreams might abate.

Crawling back in through the tent flap, he saw his sibling snuffling, clutching a crumpled photo of their mother.

"It's okay, Mikey," Alex whispered gruffly, not ashamed when his own tears began to fall.

MORNING ARRIVED with the promise of exploring the woods, followed by fishing in the afternoon. Being early October, the weather was still pleasant through the day, yet chilly in the evenings. They hiked through the vast amount of trees and were huffing by the time they reached an area which looked like an ancient burial ground.

"Wow, it's like *Pet Sematary*!"

The father scolded Alex for reading too many Stephen King books and insisted it was just some old, useless stones probably left by hippies or tree huggers.

Alex wasn't so sure. He sensed a more malevolent significance when he looked at some of the markings on the old stones.

"Bet mum would have liked it here," sniffed Mikey, looking rather forlorn.

Alex puffed his cheeks out, glancing at their father.

Mother was a taboo subject, not to be mentioned unless your life depended on it. Paul stared at his sons with a flushed face, his expression thunderous.

"I've told you, don't talk about her! And stop moping about. You're not a little kid anymore. Right, let's find this bloody river."

Heads down, the boys trudged behind their father. He wasn't a bad man, but grief had made him ugly. They didn't blame him, not really. Mikey should have known better.

Catching their own dinner and winning rare praise from Paul put pay to any spooky feelings left over from the hike, and they were soon huddled around the fire pit again, enjoying the fruits of their labour. The night had drawn in. Before long it was pitch-black, and the trio were competing to see who could yawn the loudest.

"It's the fresh air," their father told them. "No shame in admitting we're all tuckered out. Time to hit the sack I reckon."

Alex unzipped their tent and joined Mikey, noticing that he was still holding the photo of their mum, although there were no tears tonight.

"You ok, shit-for-brains?"

Smiling up at his older brother, Mikey nodded.

"I brought this with me."

Reaching under his pillow, he pulled out a silver locket that had belonged to their mother. Inside was a tiny photo of her as a baby and a lock of her hair. It smelt of lavender, just as she had.

Alex hissed and his eyes widened in surprise. "Dad'll fucking kill you if he knew you'd snuck that up here! You know he said mum's stuff is proper precious and must never leave the house!"

Snuffling, Mikey looked up at him, eyes filling again. His chest shuddered with sorrow. "I just wanted mum with us. Alex, I miss her so much. I wish she was still here. I'd give *anything* for her to be here. Anything!" He let out a sob in anguish. "I'd even die, just so she could come back. Oh, mummy..."

At that very moment, a huge gust of wind caused the tent to sway, whistling as it buffeted the sides. The night had been chilly, but the air now felt frigid. Alex shivered, not just the weather causing his skin to goosebump.

"Brrr. Come one, get snuggled down in that sleeping bag or I'll make you go in with dad and the Dreaded Farts."

Snot bubbles mixed with tears, and Mikey wiped a grubby hand across his face. Taking a deep, hitching breath, he asked, "Can you leave the lamp on, just a little?"

Alex nodded, not wanting to admit he was more than just a little spooked himself.

Before long they both nodded off...

ALEX AND MIKEY'S mother watched them sleep as she passed by their tent and over to their father, or as she now referred to him: the man who murdered her then covered it up. Before that fateful night he had always been careful to keep the beatings below the neck. No one had ever suspected such a doting husband and father could have committed such an awful crime.

Somehow, her locket had acted as a talisman and Mikey's selfless wish had been so powerful, it had turned into an incantation. The power emanating from the ancient burial ground that bastard had been so quick to dismiss was the final part in the trifecta of power that brought her vengeful spirit back.

She wouldn't touch her boys, but she would exact revenge. Entering her husband's tent, she willed herself to become corporal, just long enough to succeed in her mission. Plunging her hands into Paul's chest, she ripped at his flesh, tearing out lumps of visceral meat the deeper she dug.

STARING up at his dead wife, Paul had frozen in complete and utter terror, wanting to scream, but finding his vocal cords refused to obey. He writhed in agony as she,

it,

dug her hands into the cavity, and finally faded to black just seconds after he witnessed her holding his still beating and dripping heart...

NOT WANTING the boys waking up to find their father looking like he'd gone ten rounds with a chainsaw, she used the very last of the power from the incantation.

The pair disappeared into the unknown.

Forever.

"DAD? DAD! DAD, PLEASE ANSWER. DAD!"

Shit.

"Co-come on, M-Mikey, we have to ch-check."

Despite being petrified, Alex knew he had to look inside

the tent, especially now that the sun had risen and it was eerily silent. He hadn't been able to fall back asleep, his younger brother having drifted off into a restless slumber sometime after the noises stopped.

The boys crawled out of the tent and shakily headed over to check on their father.

Gulping, heart hammering in his chest, Alex cautiously opened the tent flap and found...

Nothing.

Not a trace of their father.

It was as if he'd simply vanished.

OF COURSE, the police searched. The boys were placed in the immediate care of their favourite aunt, their mother's sister who adored them. No longer were they afraid to talk about and celebrate her memory. They enjoyed a sad yet fulfilling childhood, despite never knowing what had become of their father. And whenever one of them was upset, they were always comforted by the distinct aroma of lavender.

The End.

Notes

Living on a Prayer (originally called *The Talisman*) was written for the Cemetery Gates Media open call for *Campfire Macabre*. I ended contributing a different story for that fantastic anthology, but still had a soft spot for this and hoped it would find its way to a good home.

There is a nod to Alex Pearson (Finding_Montayk) and Mikey is, of course, another *Goonies* reference.

It has slight *Tales from the Darkside* or *Tales from the Crypt* vibes in that revenge is enacted and the survivors end up with redemption and in a better place. I just wonder where Paul is now ...

TRACK FIFTEEN

*J*ill - *Sometimes as I sift through these papers, I have to remind myself the author is a grown woman. She seems to have a knack for capturing the mind of a teenage boy. This particular tale gave me some much-needed chuckles amongst the doom and gloom of sorting through the puzzles left with this case. And it is accurate, every town* does *have a house we invent a narrative for or equate with atrocities. And just maybe, there is a valid reason for it.*

Number 15 - Bones of Boarded-up Baby Bodies Behind the Bath-panel.

EVERY TOWN HAS ONE. A haunted house. Or to be more specific, a *reportedly* haunted house. It will be unlikely to resemble something out of a Hitchcock movie or have a roof resplendent with gargoyles and swarms of bats. Nor will it be an idling old gingerbread cottage in the woods with Mrs

Witch peering out through the boiled sweetie windows, laughing maniacally.

More often, such as the one in our town, it'll be a bog-standard end terrace that has just seen better days. The grass will come up to your knees and most of the windows will be broken and boarded up. It'll be devoid of pentagrams carved into the doorframe or dead cats nailed to the fence. Such a shame when you think about it.

No one will have lived there for years. If you were to ask one of the adults, they'd get this pinched look on their face and suggest that they can't remember and that they are *very busy, dear so why don't you run along now?*

If you ask one of the older kids, they'll tell you it's used as a den of iniquity, for a quick grope or a lucky shag. That *they've* been there. And did you know Jennifer Muller gave out blowjobs on Friday nights?

The middle teens will regale you with tales of gang initiation and no, I'm not talking Mafia stuff. This is Somerset, not Goodfella's. 'Gang' in this instance refers to a rag-bag group of 14-year-old boys who think they're hard because they nicked one of their dad's McEwan's and a couple of Lambert and Butler. Rather than execution style shots to the head, they sneak off together to some home-made bodge job of a den so they can look at Page 3 girls in The Sun whilst trying not to jizz in their He-Man boxers. And the initiation? Daring each other to break into the house and bring back a trophy. A piece of bone, a torn strip of bloody material, the handle of a well-used hammer...none of those things had ever been retrieved on one of the outings. At most they'd find a used johnnie or a pair of skanky knickers from one of the sixth formers.

But boring truths never get in the way of rumours, the gossip, the campfire tales – if we did shit like that in good ol'

Blighty. Well, I guess maybe if you were a Cub or something. I digress.

And what would be the point even of a good old fashioned creepy house, if everyone didn't have some story about who had lived there, about why it was now dilapidated and abandoned, and a conviction that only theirs was the correct version. Over the years, I had heard the following:

The mum had gone bonkers and killed all her babies, stuffing them behind the bath panel.

The dad liked to fuck little boys and made one of the bedrooms into a sex dungeon.

The kid had gone full on Lizzie Borden.

The family were cannibals and ate themselves…

Yeah, that last one was a bit far-fetched, even for us 12-year-olds.

Every Halloween, that house was the King Pin, the lottery, the jackpot, despite there being no one there to give out sweets or tell us to *fuck off, this is England you little shits*. Every Trick or Treat pilgrimage would end up there. More often than not, you'd just stand and stare at the house. You never needed to actually cross the threshold to feel your bowels begin to loosen. Just from being in its mere presence, you could sense the malevolence oozing from the very foundations. Seeping over you, coating you in a thin, invisible layer of wrong.

My mate Scotty and I knew there was something fucked up in that house. We drove ourselves and the other lads nuts over it. Did our teachers head's in as we were always talking about it. We were obsessed. But we were both pussies too. I can admit that now. I couldn't even tell you how many times we rode our bikes over there and just stood, gawping at it.

Never quite brave enough to breach the non-existent barrier barring us from entering.

As I have mentioned, this wasn't some derelict building, some in the middle of nowhere run-down old manor house. This was a shitty old 'no one knew why it had been abandoned or who even owned it now' property on a normal boring street in the middle of a busy working-class town in the heart of Somerset. People noticed us. It must have been bloody annoying at best and damn right intrusive at worst, an invasion of privacy to be honest. But we were kids.

This was back before people bothered to call the Old Bill at the slightest hint of trouble. Mainly because they probably knew your parents and with just one word to your dad, you wouldn't be able to walk for a week. Or the neighbours would just come out and clip you around the ear before telling you to bugger off. Different times. But like bees to a honey pot, that just made it all the more seductive. The interior of the dwelling may have been empty, but just being in the vicinity was enough to feed our pre-teen imaginations and fuel our nightmares.

Every sleepover, every bike ride, *every* break time watching the other boys knock a footy around (jumpers for goalposts), we would plot how to get into that house. You would have thought we were planning to rob the Crown Jewels. But I never for one moment thought that we would actually do it...

It's sort of like when you lose your virginity. The build-up of how great it'll be, all those frantic wanks in the bathroom imagining the act. Then, in reality when it actually happens...it's over in seconds and you're always a bit let down. Anticipation is everything. Plus, as aforementioned, we were both total pussies. We'd never *really* break in there. In all reality, the place was probably littered with shit, actual shit. Dirt and filth. Old, mouldy cans, used needles. The stories we heard, and the ones we created, would always be better than what truthfully lay behind those walls.

So, when Scotty appeared outside my window one Saturday evening and I couldn't think of a decent enough excuse not to creep out of my room and join him, we found ourselves headed to Chez Munster's once again. Only this time, there seemed a sense of urgency. I couldn't quite put my finger on it, but it just felt…different.

No sooner had we arrived and dumped our bikes on the kerb then Scotty looked me in the eye and said, "We're going in."

It wasn't an invite or a challenge. There was no *maybe* about it. This was happening. Right now. Go straight to jail, do not pass go.

His odd sense of calm and devil-may-care attitude should have buoyed me on. He had progressed from co-captain to leader with ease, and I needed to be a willing follower. To be honest, it had all happened so quickly, I'm not even sure I was thinking straight. The yellowed grass came past his bony knees as he strode confidently around to the back of the house. Of course, I followed. No way was I being left outside like some sort of bellend. As much as I didn't want to go *in*, being the leftover seemed even worse somehow.

Despite my legging it round the back after him, Scotty was almost through the kitchen window by the time I got there. I heard a grunt as he landed on the other side and realised this was it. No backsies now. Double Dog Dare. Gingerly I reached up to the ledge and hauled my body through the opening. Of course, Mr Tosspot here would be the one to nick his hand on the rusty nail sticking out of the wall on the way in. Now, even if nothing else happened, I'd have to dob and tell mum or risk infection. Bet she'd make me go for a tetanus and I knew that meant a giant needle in my arse. Fucking perfect.

And just like that, with both no prior planning and having planned for it for the last five years, we were inside, actually inside, the house. My heart was hammering in my chest, my breath hitching as I tried in desperation to remember I was not being held against my will. I wanted this.

Predictably, it was just as filthy and disgusting as I had imagined. I had a distinct feeling that I would have to burn my clothes – the stench already having seeped into the material. I licked my lips, tasting salt and something else. Not having remotely intended to be partaking of some urbex, I was poorly equipped. I'd barely had time to shove some jeans and a sweater over my PJs. Scotty however brought a torch, so we were able to stumble through the detritus covering the rotting carpet tiles and exposed floorboards. Not that I actually wanted to see whatever was running across the cesspit or the face containing those tiny, red eyes in the corner. As we meandered through the lower level of the property, taking in the surroundings and trying desperately to commit every single nook and cranny to memory, I felt the sudden urge to ask Scotty why we were there. Why now? Of all the times we had spoken about it, why had he suddenly decided that he could wait no longer? Why was tonight do or die?

Unsurprisingly, he didn't have any profound revelations about how someone had come to him in a dream, or he had some bombastic epiphany. He just stared at me, ignored the question and began to head up the stairs.

Okay then.

I was about halfway up, placing my feet on the edge of each step so as to not plunge through the wood, when the smell hit me. I say smell, but it was full on rancid stench. If I'd thought the rot, mould, damp and bodily fluids downstairs was bad, I ain't seen, or in this case inhaled, nothing yet.

It may seem like hyperbole, but I could literally taste the noxiousness of it. The air felt thick as it permeated my dermis, and I knew I would never feel total sanitation again. Scotty appeared unperturbed, or he at least didn't give any acknowledgement to the malodour, which again just wasn't right.

"Bloody hell," I said nasally as I had pinched my thumb and forefinger on my nose, closing my nostrils, "what in the actual fuck is that stink?"

Scotty stopped dead in front of me and I almost bowled into him. I saw him, via the dim light emitting from his torch, shrug his shoulders in a nonchalant or even uninterested fashion.

"Dunno," he replied, although it wasn't necessary. His body language had answered in lieu.

To be honest, he was starting to piss me off. Until then, I had been fuelled by adrenaline alone. The excitement, anticipation and sheer audacity of breaking in had pushed me on, overcoming fear, common sense and better judgement. Now, however, those negative feelings were breaking the surface, overruling any exhilaration. Especially since Scotty was being such a tosser.

As we ascended the stairs, the landing delivered the grand prize of...three closed doors. I prophesied two would be bedrooms, the last a bathroom – the latter being a likely source of the revolting smell. It would have been years since any plumbing and pipes in the house were in working order. God only knows what might be in that toilet or bath. And if the rumours about the bones of boarded-up baby bodies behind the bath panel were true...

Even with the miserable dribble of light Scotty's torch was emitting, the darkness up here was on a whole other level. Granted, it was because all the doors were closed, and where there should have been a landing window, the glass had long ago been smashed and cheap MDF nailed across it. Although I thought my eyes had begun to adjust to it, now I may as well have been blindfolded. It heightened the already trepidatious scenario ten-fold.

I felt my voice tremble as I asked, "So, pick a door any door. Which is it to be, number 1, 2 or 3?" God I could be hilarious when I wanted to be.

The usual Scotty would have pissed himself even though it wasn't actually that funny, slapped me on the back whilst stating, "good one!" This new and unimproved version of my best mate didn't even acknowledge my quip. He merely strode over to the middle door, pushing it open without hesitation.

If I had thought I could taste the stink before, it now felt as though I was bathing in it. I gagged, a little bit of sick rising up into my mouth. What in the actual fuck could be in that room? Despite being only 12 and incredibly naive, I was pretty sure that it couldn't actually be the rotting, bloated, violated corpses of young boys that the father of the house had used and abused for his own sickening sexual pleasures. *If*, and it was a huge if, that was true, the police would have removed all evidence. I *knew* that. Same for if the alleged former child of the property had channelled their inner Ripper tendencies and butchered their parents, there wouldn't be any actual cadavers here now. Worst case scenario, a cat had crawled in here to die. Yes, that made total sense! It would be gross and stinky but still only some fetid feline.

As I watched Scotty disappear into the room, I told myself to man up and follow him, prove to myself more than anything that I wasn't a total fucking loser. Hell, if there was something to use in there, I'd even give that mangy moggy a poke, see if any maggots came up! Yeah!

So, I followed him in. Well, to the threshold of the door anyway.

Through the darkness, Scotty's weak beam loitered on something on the floor. Something that immediately didn't feel right. The rest of the house was barren aside from rubbish left by lazy teens. Even squatters didn't stay in this place for long. There had been no furniture in any room so far, so what the hell was that large lump?

"Wh-what is that, Scotty?" I stammered, unsure that I actually wanted to know, and yet needing to at the same time.

No answer.

"Sc-Scotty?" Gulping, insides churning like a milkmaid making butter, I meandered over to join him. Now that I was closer, I saw the pathetic torch light was indeed illuminating just enough of the lump to garner what in fact it was.

Specifically, he had lit up the end of the thing closest to the wall. And with the beam trained on that one area it became clear as day and yet as unclear as night what we were looking at.

A dead body.

A very specific dead body belonging to a very specific

and instantly recognisable person. It made no sense and every sense all at once.

As I stood there, bile rising, bladder loosening I had only one question.

"Scotty?"

...

The End.

Notes

This was another occasion where the plot just came to me and I just sat and wrote, letting the words flow. This story thrived with the 80s non-social media frenzy setting and yes again, the voice is in part a British male teenager. It does seem to be my favourite, probably as I get to use words like tosser and bellend and at the end of the day, I have a rather juvenile sense of humour.

The finale scene is quite ironic as I have already pointed out that I loathe ambiguous open endings myself. Cannot stand them in fact and yet...

What do *you* think happened?

TRACK SIXTEEN

Jill - If, like me, you choose to read this at bedtime, you might need to sleep with the light on ... and maybe a Tylenol. This tale features what I think is one of the more frightening subject matters – dreams...

Number 16 - Nobody's Fool.

A LOT of new parents could win first prize at a Mumm-Ra cosplay contest. This was the case in our house for certain. We never got much sleep. You see our son, Axl, had horrific nightmares. When he was very young, the doctors told us they were night terrors, and he would grow out of it. They assured us it wasn't unusual for preschoolers to wet the bed and writhe around in their sheets as if battling terrifying monsters.

But Axl didn't grow out of them. As *he* grew, so did his

imagination. Instead of improving, the dreams got worse. Far, far worse.

We tried everything. Anything that could be deemed as scary – books, TV shows, movies – were banned. No *Scooby-Doo* or *Dark Crystal* allowed. R L Stine was persona non grata. Usual childhood fears were debunked, like how there was no Boogeyman or monsters under the bed. Plausible scenarios were addressed but with solid solutions. Yes, there were bad people in the world, but we had a top-of-the-line security system, so a break-in was impossible. We left lights on, read happy and peaceful stories, played ambient music. Tried meditation, mindfulness. My wife even co-slept, to see if feeling safe and secure wrapped in her arms would make a difference.

But night after night, he would wake, bathed in sweat, exuding terror from every pore. Nothing could calm him, he'd just scream and scream until he was hoarse, rocking himself as he re-lived over and over the atrocities in his mind.

Next, was counselling. Drawing crude crayon pictures of what he imagined. The therapist was disturbed. We faced many awkward questions about what we let him watch, or the topics of conversation he was subjected to. But we couldn't figure out the origin. We didn't watch that kind of stuff. Neither of us liked horror or gore; we were both kind of squeamish. We didn't own any crime books or watch cop shows. Well, maybe something like Columbo now and again, but that wasn't R rated, and Axl would have been in bed anyway. Stephen King and Thomas Harris just weren't part of our world.

Although sickening, the question of abuse arose. It was well known that sometimes kids invent monsters to represent perceived reality, to try to explain what is happening. We consented to him being examined and asked appropriate questions about touching. But, thank god, there was no evidence of any kind. Nothing, zip, nada. Despite the tremendous relief, it still left us baffled. What the hell *was* feeding his imagination?

In the end, they prescribed medication. He was thirteen years old, but the lack of sleep over the years had affected him so severely (his appetite, his growth, stamina), he looked about ten. Small and skinny, pale enough to resemble one of the ghouls from his dreams. Drugging him seemed the most viable option.

And...it worked. Whether he stopped *having* the dreams, or just didn't remember them, we'd never know. What was important was that he slept. There might be side-effects of the medication of course, but wasn't there always? He was already withdrawn and sullen; years of terror never quite allowed him to fully recharge his batteries. The fact he might present even more like a zombie was still better than the alternative.

It had all come to a head when he started to tell the counsellor about The End. We were stunned. No matter how morose he had been, we never imagined he might be suicidal. Yet, he was adamant that there was to be an 'End' and that life would be over.

As a parent, nothing prepares you for that. You'd do anything to take away those thoughts and feelings from the person you love more than anything. It broke our hearts.

"16!" He would scream at the top of his lungs upon waking each night.

"16, 16, 16!"

We would rush to him, take him in our arms like when

he was little, abate the terror with parental love, for all the good it did. When questioned, he couldn't answer or elaborate. Just the same story, over and over – life must end.

And so, it seemed that the dreams and the drawings had become dangerous enough that medication was the most humane alternative.

FOR A WHILE, life became, well...better. Alongside sleep, Axl's concentration and health improved. He started getting decent grades, made a few friends. Started to enjoy life, to some extent anyway.

Counselling remained mandatory. Even though the dreams had been removed, the memories still existed, as did the question of why they had occurred in the first place. As he got older – we blamed hormones – he got more and more angry during sessions. I think it was pure frustration on his part. He didn't *know* why he'd had the dreams; couldn't they just move on and accept that?

He became more agitated the closer it got to his birthday. Although the medication still knocked him out at bedtime, enabling him to sleep, he awoke each morning with those dark circles under his eyes and the same pallor from when he had been having his 'episodes.'.

The school had been in touch. He was failing classes. His behaviour had become erratic, disruptive. The few friends began drifting away.

Therapy was met with a wall of silence. He simply sat there, staring at nothing, refusing to engage with the counsellor he had known for years. A vacant expression painted upon his face, eyes blank and unseeing. Changing his medication was suggested.

The final days leading up to his birthday were the worst. He had become even more withdrawn. Didn't eat. Spent all day and night in bed, yet couldn't sleep, even with the pills. The night before his Big Day (he might not have wanted it, but a surprise party awaited him) he turned, looking right at me for the first time in days. I was sitting on the end of the bed when his voice jolted me out of my stupor.

"Dad," he croaked, his voice sounding husky from lack of use. "I'm sorry. I...I couldn't stop them."

"Stop who, son?" I replied. "Stop what?"

But he refused to engage anymore. Then, just before midnight, his eyelids drooping, he muttered, "I love you and Mom."

Heart breaking, I kissed the top of his head and went to bed.

I THINK the shit hit the fan sometime around 2am. As it was night-time, I didn't realise the power was out right away. What woke me was the smashing and horrific screaming from outside.

"What the –" I mumbled, semi-falling out of the bed and stumbling to the window. The darkness made it hard to determine what was occurring. That's when I noted the streetlights were off. I could just make out shadows and outlines due to the moon.

Oh, and the fires.

Yes, it looked like the entire world was on fire. People were crying, howling. Cars crashing in their driver's haste. And the noise. That awful, terrifying noise. Ripping, tearing, wetness...

And fuck, the smell! Like BBQ or when my wife caught

her hair on a candle; the acrid aroma of... burning, charring flesh.

Panic rose in my throat, self-preservation kicking in. I shook my wife awake and then raced towards Axl's room without waiting to explain what the fuck was going on.

"We need to leave now!" I shouted towards Axl's door. "Get out of the house, get to the car!"

But it was too late. Whilst I'd been concentrating on what was happening outside, I had neglected to check what might be *inside*. Or hear it racing up the stairs.

"No," I heard my wife scream, before it ripped off her head. Frozen in shock, I watched her blood repaint the white bedroom walls she'd been so fond of.

Out of the corner of my eye, I could see Axl, standing by his door.

Dropping to my knees as it leapt, I accepted my fate.

"Happy Sweet 16, son," I managed, before it tore me in two.

Caked in viscera, it screamed in victory, the sound echoing throughout the land as others joined it.

"16," Axl whispered. "16."

WANDERING THE STREETS, he barely reacted to the atrocities surrounding him. There was utter carnage everywhere. Had he ever seen *The Evil Dead* he might have made comparisons, but he didn't even know such a thing existed. Except for in his dreams...

Until now.

He walked, ignoring the humans being split apart, the children being dismembered, their parents watching in horror before joining the ever-growing piles of burning body parts. Where he was headed wasn't clear, but one thing in all the chaos was apparent. Whilst every other living thing was being eviscerated, claws and teeth too quick for any self-defence, Axl remained untouched. A few people noticed and tried to get his attention before their eyes were gouged out or tongues ripped from their throats, though whether it was to plead for help or give a warning wasn't clear. It didn't matter; he saw and heard nothing.

The boy continued alone, bypassing the ever-increasing funeral pyres, headed north. It took a week before he decided to rest. He was unsure of how much terrain he had covered in that time; the city had become fields and woodlands and rivers. There were fewer and fewer survivors now to notice him, not that he ever paid any attention to sound or sight. Axl just kept walking, repeating the same mantra over and over...

"16. 16. 16."

The End.

Notes

The premise behind this story is simple. I heard something of a similar vein but with the main character as a patient on a psychiatric ward. They would end each visit with their partner counting down numbers, until they got to one and we were led to believe something happened, but the ending was left open...

I liked this idea so decided to create my own version but with a kid, dreams and an apocalypse of sorts. Are they walkers a la *The Walking Dead*? Aliens? Or something even worse.

The boy was originally called Adam, but since I had a prominent character in this collection already with that name, I changed it to Axl. That is an homage to Mr Rose and Master Rolfe.

TRACK SEVENTEEN

J*ill – well here we are, the final story in the collection. I feel privileged to have been the one to discover these lost works and am thrilled to have been able to share them with you. As with any compilation, there may be stories you prefer, others just not your cup of tea. But hopefully there will be something for everybody. I get the sense that the author was proud of each and every tale, but there are one or two where her love for the plot and characters shone through above others. It seemed fitting to save this one for last, as I could tell it was a favourite of hers.*

Reminiscent of a more innocent time when a kiss on the cheek from a crush and beating your mates in a bravery contest was everything. Thank you for reading along with me.

Number 17 - They

KIDS.

Kids and animals.

Bloody interfering self-righteous kids and animals. Never work with them *they* say

(who the hell are *they* anyway?)

They always know *they* say. If a kid or an animal doesn't trust someone, neither should you. They're the best judge of character.

Well, fuck that.

I've fooled them all ...

IT STARTED when I was 11 years old. 1988. Man, those were the days. School was easy. Reading and writing, basic addition and subtraction. That was the extent of pressure we had on us. The rest of the day was painting, playing the recorder, climbing the apparatus in the gym. Pretending to be Hulk Hogan anytime we were on the playground.

Bliss.

Sure, the cook would walk around, brandishing her wooden spoon with malicious intent if you didn't eat all your dubious-looking meat and potato slop. But the chocolate sponge with mint custard made up for that.

After school was a hazy mix of knocking for friends, being called in for tea (mum's homemade pizza was the best) when it got dark and waiting for the TV to 'warm up' so you could watch your favourite cartoon (*Thundercats*, obviously).

Then bath, bed (pretending to go to sleep, but reading *The Hardy Boys* with a torch under the covers) before starting all over again the next day.

My parents were well, normal, working in the bank and

at my school. We weren't well off but were far from being on the breadline. Weekends we visited grandparents and played with cousins. Sometimes dad took me to the footy. Otherwise, I was out on my bike with my mates most of the day. That was just the way that life was.

Until one day in 1988 when everything changed.

IT WAS an early Sunday morning in December. You know the type - cold and drizzling, a dull and dark day. But we were 11 years old and invincible. We didn't care about getting wet! Who gives a crap about soggy trainers when you're with your best mates? Anyway, we had shell-suits and raincoats. We could do anything.

We rode off across the fields as always. The warning of 'try to be back by lunch time!' (or when our tummies were rumbling) ringing in our ears. Knowing where we were headed.

The storm drains.

Large concrete cylindrical tunnels that ran the length of the stream in the field opposite our houses. The outside was covered in crude graffiti. I don't know who poor Sally was, but someone thought she was a 'total slag'.

Looking back now, it was foolish and dangerous. But you don't think about stuff like that at the time. We would dare each other to run through it. See who was the fastest. Who could stay in there, in the middle where it was pitch black, the longest. I had made it for five minutes once. That was until I felt a small, chittering body scamper over my foot. I may have been foolhardy, but there was no way I was going home with rat bites!

We drove ourselves mad making up stories of what might be in that tunnel.

Killer clowns.

Giant flesh-eating newts.

Even zombie cats who would lure you with a cute meow and then eat your brains. Young lads have brilliant yet overactive imaginations.

That day in particular, there was a very special prize on offer for who could stay there the longest. We had an extra member in our party, a VIP for one-time only. Cassie, the 12-year-old cousin of my neighbour, Scott, was here for the day and we were all a little bit in love with her. She was a total babe, with ginger pigtails and the most adorable dimples when she smiled. We were yet to be all-consumed by raging hormones, and most girls were not worth our time, but Cassie was a 12-year-old Goddess. The prize for whom was to be deemed the bravest, was a kiss on the cheek. This had already blown our 11-year-old minds, so we were feeling especially courageous that day.

Since it was a storm drain and there had been consistent rain for the last few days, needless to say the water inside was at a reasonable level. It never got dangerous, but it was nevertheless, at least ankle deep, with some parts almost reaching your knees. We were only short too, being a mix of 10- and 11-year-old boys, not quite yet at puberty and sudden growth spurts.

One by one, we ventured into the drain. The first to try, Scott, only lasted around thirty seconds. In his defence, Cassie was his cousin, and he would rather have died than receive a kiss on the cheek from her. Trying next, was Luke. Being the youngest, he lasted nighty-three seconds. He was doing alright until he tripped, fell on his arse and realised he would be spending the next few hours with soggy *He-Man* pants.

After Luke, came my sole competition. Ashley had managed four minutes forty-three seconds on his previous attempt. He'd rushed out, having claimed to have heard a low growling noise and thought a dog might have gotten in. We said it was more likely to be his stomach; he was never seen without a Club biscuit or a Wham bar in his pocket.

This time however, same as I, he was buoyed by the promise of a kiss from an 'older woman'. That sort of thing made you feel invincible. So, with a wink in Cassie's direction (I was overjoyed to see her roll her eyes at that) he sped off into the abyss.

And we waited.

And waited.

The hands on her Mickey Mouse watch seemed to be speeding, as if somehow in cahoots with Ashley to make time go faster. Four minutes came and went. Four and a half. I was beginning to sweat despite the cool air and the drizzling rainfall.

Five minutes.

God damn it, he now held my record.

At five minutes nineteen, we heard a noise. It was muffled, so Ashley must have been quite far in, but it was definitely a sort of yelp. Then, we heard splashing and at exactly five minutes and twenty-seven seconds, he came tearing out of the pipe.

Panting.

Looking like shit.

"What's up, Ash?" I asked." Did your guts start talking to you again, haha?"

Looking up at me from where he had dropped to the floor, he glared.

"Fuck off" was the reply. "It weren't my guts. There's summat in there, I swear!"

Of course, we all laughed at him. 'Cause that's what kids do, right? He was proper pissed off and sulked for a bit before turning to glare at me.

"Alright then Sammy, *you* go in and try to beat me. I'm still way in the lead."

I scoffed at him. Beat five minutes twenty-seven? Easy. I was aiming for closer to ten. Sneaking a look at Cassie, she smiled back. Blushing, I wiped my hand over my sodden face. This was it.

Later, suckers.

And in I went.

BECAUSE WE HADN'T BEEN in there for a few weeks, and the rain had been so relentless, the usual dank smell had worsened ten-fold. As I neared the middle of the tunnel and thus the deeper water, the stench made me gag. *Bloody hell, it stinks*! I thought, like when the cat had brought in a headless rat one day and hidden it under one of the kitchen cupboards. The house had reeked, and dad had to remove all the kickboards until he found its rotting corpse. That's what it was like in the tunnel, only worse.

Much worse.

Hurrying, I stumbled on a little further than usual, trying to escape the smell. Maybe a tramp crawled in here to escape the cold and took a dump? Keeping my feet to the sides as much as possible, I aimed to avoid soaking my trainers. It occurred to me that I was now venturing into a part of the drain thus far undiscovered. Virgin territory if you will. You see, the other end of the pipe was obscured by trees and even small animals would have trouble squeezing through the branches and then negotiating the grating. We were lucky that our end was open, and the original grate had been broken, so we were able to crawl through the space with ease.

As the other end remained shut, there was very little light emitted into the tunnel. And on a dank day like today, the darkness oozed like a living thing.

I stopped suddenly. I had lost my footing just enough and slipped. My trainers stirred up the water underneath and the stench rose again. But it wasn't the smell that had me frozen. It was the sound. A low, guttural growling. I held my breath. *It's all in your mind, it's all in your mind.* I was just thinking about what bloody Ashley had said. There was *nothing* in here that could growl. Even my damn cat couldn't squeeze though that grate on the other side, let alone a dog.

Pull yourself together, you pussy! I had no idea how long I'd been in there now, but it must have been more than Ashely. Long enough that my eyes were starting to adjust to the darkness. So, I could just make out a strange shape in the water.

A sort of...lump.

A sort of large, dark lump with a big 'thing' sticking out of it which I of course managed to trip over. Completely losing my already precarious balance, I landed straight onto said 'lump' and into the fetid water.

"Fucks sake!" I yelled in desperation, trying to scramble to my feet, finding it difficult to grab anything that wasn't slippery to give myself some purchase.

That was when I heard the noise again. This time, the low snarling was much clearer. And far nearer. I wanted to scream but alas, when I tried, nothing would come out. It was like my vocal cords were frozen in fear, just like my body.

Then I saw them. Approaching me

(quickly)

from the far end of the tunnel.

Eyes.

(run)

Two yellow, glowing orbs. I think I might have pissed myself at that point, but to be honest, I was that wet, I didn't care.

My heart was beating so fast I thought I was going into cardiac arrest. And then, the *thing* pounced. It pinned me to the floor of the tunnel, those bright, yellow eyes staring right into mine. I could feel its malodorous breath on my face. Nausea rose in my throat as I wondered what was going to kill me? Choking on my own vomit? Drowning in this putrid drain water? Or being ripped apart by whatever the fuck was standing on my chest.

Then, it opened its enormous mouth, revealing so many teeth I knew right there and then, that I was a goner...

"Sam! Sam? SAM!"

"What?" Hearing my name being called, I couldn't quite place where it was coming from.

Feeling groggy, I winced as I sat up. Rubbed my eyes. Eugh. That's when I realised, I was still lying in the storm drain.

Funny, I thought, *I could have sworn I was much further in?*

I could see some light and the edge of our opening. Hadn't I been much closer to the opposite gate?

I looked up again, noticing a shadow blocking the light. It looked like a person.

"Sam? What are you doing in there, mate? Sam!"

"Huh?" I tried to stand up, legs like jelly. Splash and "ouch" as I fell down, hard onto my butt.

"Fuck it, I'm going in." I heard. Footsteps and then Scott, looking down at me.

"What the –" he asked while peering closely at me. "Mate, you look like you're covered in shit. And you've been in here ages! We waited 'til Cassie's watch said fifteen minutes then we started to call to you. Ash swore he could still hear that weird growling noise too."

Putting his hands under my armpits, he lifted me up.

"Were you just taking the piss or did summat happen in here?"

I looked down at where I had been lying. No strange lump.

"Um, I was, erm..." I looked behind me, shivering.

"I was just messing with you. Haha. Gotcha! I get that kiss now, don't I?"

"You dick," laughed Scott and we walked out together, me trying not to wince as I put weight on my ankle.

"I did slip," I admitted, "and I think there's rats in there. Fucking stinks."

Cassie sidled over to me. She wrinkled her nose (I did hum) but dutifully placed a kiss upon my cheek.

We had a bit of a laugh about what a twat I was, and then biked back home. We were all drenched and most of us were covered in crap.

My head was spinning. And my body felt like I had been run over by a train.

Mum took one look at me, shook her head and shoved me in the bath. I was covered in the usual cuts and bruises for an 11-year-old boy. What do you expect when you ride across fields on a beat-up old bike, climb trees and play in storm drains?

Rolling her eyes at the state of me, I was instructed to have a good soak, whilst she decided whether to try to wash my filthy clothes or just burn them.

I winced as I lay down in the warm, soapy tub. There was one cut on the back of my right shoulder which was killing me. It wasn't bleeding, but it felt raw.

But mostly, my mind was racing. What the hell had happened in that tunnel? It was coming back to me in fits and bursts. But the part that seemed to make no sense at all and yet, was of the up-most importance was, what the fuck had those teeth belonged to?

It wasn't until a few weeks later that what happened, came back to bite me in the arse.

Daytime had been fine. There was the buzz of pre-Christmas excitement in the air and the constant chatter of which new gadgets and games we were hoping to find under the tree. I busied myself as much as possible with helping mum and dad – making mince pies, decorating the tree, digging out the old rusty sledge just in case there was snow.

My mates and I hadn't talked much about that day. In fact, the thing that had caused the most excitement (and both equal embarrassment and smugness) was The Kiss. There were lots of smoothing sounds and chants of "Sam and Cassie sitting in the tree, K I S S I N G." She was due to visit over the holidays and to Scott's annoyance, wouldn't stop talking about me.

It would have been the best few weeks of my life, if it weren't for the dreams …

I hadn't stopped thinking, or dreaming, about those eyes.

And those teeth.

So.

Many.

Teeth …

I hadn't dared go back to the drains. Thank god, the weather had been even shitter than usual. Our mums were happy to keep us in, or at least, for us to stick to racing up and down the paths in front of the houses.

It happened that night. I can't really explain to you what it feels like. Imagine the worst pain you have ever experienced. Perhaps, you've broken a bone. Or, had a nasty cut where you've had to pull something out, like glass. Well, quadruple that and you are still nowhere near this excruciating agony.

Basically, every bone in my entire body broke and somehow, manipulated itself until reaching its desired non-human shape.

Limbs elongated, skin ripped apart, as the new cartilage forced its way through my flesh.

Fingernails shed, as claws appeared at the end of my huge, hairy hands.

I think the worst, even more so than my spine bending, was my jaw breaking and stretching. Fangs broke through my gums with piercing, mind-numbing force, and I spat out a bucketful of blood, and teeth.

At last, I understood what I had encountered in the storm drain ...

I don't actually remember much about what I did that night. The morning after is always, thankfully, hazy at best. But I do know, the priority was to go back into the dark, rank tunnel. Somehow, I knew that there would be more strange lumps waiting for me. Only the first few changes though.

Then, I understood, I would have to hunt for my own.

I AM 15 NOW. The year is 1992 and I am doing alright in secondary school. English is my best subject. The teachers say I have a very good imagination, especially when it comes to making up scary stories. I try to keep the violence to a minimum. The work is a lot harder but break and lunch time make up for it. These days it's all about kicking a ball around rather than pretending to be pro-wrestlers. We get a bit more attention from the ladies that way too.

Cassie still comes to visit Scott every so often and I have managed to get a little bit more than a kiss on the cheek from her. It's a shame she doesn't live any closer. Those pigtails are now a short, sleek bob. The dimples still drive me mad. I would forsake footie with the lads at lunch for a hand-job behind the bike sheds with her.

It helps that I am pretty ripped for someone who has just reached their mid-teens. I am physically strong and very fit. Must be all that iron and protein ...

Mum and dad are still fine. We had a slight upset when we 'lost' the cat. They never did find her. That was actually a mistake. She shouldn't have followed me out that night though. There are no exceptions when I'm hungry.

The town is still pretty boring.

Not a lot happens.

We do have some interest from time to time. Around once a month, someone's pet or occasionally some*one* (to be fair, a person who won't be missed at first) seems to just ... disappear.

Then to add to the mystery, it always happens during a full moon. Fancy that ...

I've still got loads of mates. Thanks to Cassie, a sort-of girlfriend. And we got a new cat. They all fucking love me. So, it's not always true what 'they say'. Sometimes *they* are wrong. You shouldn't always trust a child or animal's opinion of someone.

'Cause whilst they all think I'm amazing (even the cat sleeps on my bed), little do they know that once a month, I am just waiting for an excuse to rip their fucking throat out...

The End.

Notes

This story is extremely important to me. It is one of my earlier works (and my first werewolf story) and although the plot never changed, it was edited for grammar and clauses etc. by Graeme Reynolds and reads far more smoothly from that second pair of experienced eyes.

It is also the first story I ever sent to *my* favourite author and creator of the phenomenal foreword for this collection, Glenn Rolfe. His reply was as follows –

"Just read *They*...and I loved it! Great job! It's fantastic."

(Yes, I did cry.)

Then, a few months later, Glenn asked me to submit a

story for his Alien Agenda Publishing sampler. I still hadn't found anywhere to home *They*, so I asked if he would maybe like it and of course, he said yes!

I owe Glenn more than he'll ever know. Inspiration. Influence. Advice. Admiration. Mentorship and most importantly - friendship.

TRIGGER WARNINGS

Overall profanity, gore, violence, sexual content, child abuse. Stories 1, 5, 7 and 12 considered splatterpunk.

1. Menstrual bleeding
2. Kidnap
3. Kidnap and torture
4. Inference of child abuse/child sexual abuse. Child death
5. Explicit sexual content with adults. Gore
6. .
7. Obsession and stalking. Sexual scenes and gore. Decapitation
8. Inference of child death, cannibalism
9. Inference of child abuse. Child death
10. Murder
11. Attempted sexual assault
12. Explicit sexual content involving teen boys. Gore. Genital mutilation
13. Inference of child abuse/child sexual abuse/suicide

14. Inference of spousal abuse
15. Child death
16. Mental health
17. .

Spotify Playlist

1. Hungry like the Wolf – Duran Duran
2. When Doves Cry - Prince
3. I want to Break Free - Queen
4. Maneater – Hall and Oates
5. Addicted to Love – Robert Palmer
6. Sweet Child O' Mine – Guns N' Roses
7. Tainted Love – Soft Cell
8. Lost in the Shadows – Lou Gramm - The Lost Boy's Soundtrack
9. It's a Sin – Pet Shop Boys
10. Love is a Battlefield – Pat Benatar
11. Running with the Devil – Van Halen
12. Paradise City – Guns N' Roses
13. School's out for Summer … - Alice Cooper
14. Livin' on a Prayer – Bon Jovi
15. Thriller – Michael Jackson
16. Nobody's Fool – Cinderella
17. Thundercats Theme Tune

ACKNOWLEDGMENTS

There are so many people I want to mention, and I just know I'll forget someone. But here we go, in no particular order.

Thank you to –

My husband and daughter. My rocks, my life, my soul. I love you both, always.

Glenn, for rising from the ranks of favourite writer to mentor and most importantly, friend. You inspire and influence me more than you'll ever know.

Hunter, for being the person I would most like to hang out with. You are not only an amazing writer but bloody hilarious and a great friend.

Tim, for encouraging and supporting me, and trusting me with your words. Your friendship means so much.

Jason, for making me laugh and being genuinely helpful and supportive. You allowed me in to your 'crew' and I feel blessed to be a part of the family.

Jack, fellow Red Sox fan and vampire lover – you just rock.

Jill, there will never be enough or the right words to

express how thankful I am and how much I love you. BFF's forever. Love you muchly.

Lou, who'd have thought us pair of wallies would end up with a podcast? Thank you for being an amazing bestie and correcting my rogue commas over and over …

Sadie, we all need a mother figure at the helm, supporting and encouraging us and you are that figure and so much more. You have been integral in my journey and growth as a writer and person. I love you.

Cameron, you are way high on my list of favourite people for a reason. You're always there for me and I adore you.

Kenzie, my splatterpunk bestie, you have allowed me to let out and embrace my love of the extreme. You bring out my darker and sillier side and I love it.

Holli, you are a huge inspiration to me whether you know it or not. You've spent so much time thanking me for helping you out, but you are the kind of writer I can only ever dream of being.

Ben, review and buddy-read bestie, we've had some fun and you helped bring back a joy to reviewing and interviewing again. You're going places...

Andrew, the amount of faith you've put in me and the ridiculous and endless things you've done to support my writing are just incredible. I hope one day you go into PR and make a fortune.

Josh, one day we'll be supping Dunkin together and I cannot wait. Your support and true friendship will never be forgotten.

Graeme, for paying it forward with advice and helping more than you'll ever know. Everyone needs a first boost from someone who doesn't take any crap.

Brian Moreland, for helping, supporting, inspiring and

being a bloody good friend. You have a heart of gold and the talent of King.

Brian Keene, having someone as talented and supportive as you on my side is a true *pinch me* moment. You're a master of horror for a reason and I'm grateful to the core to have you here with me.

If you have supported me in anyway shape or form, please just know how grateful I am.

To all my patrons – sometimes I feel like a fraud for even having patrons but you all rock and don't know how much your support means to me.

Also thank you to all my beta readers –
Lou Yardley
Joshua Marsella
Rowan Hill
Emily Haynes
Elford Alley
Stephen Howard
Jen Snow
Jennifer Soucey
Donnie Goodman
Kenzie Jennings
Justin Montgomery
Ronaldo Katwaro
J C Robinson
Michael Fowler
James Newman
Andrew – Skeletons with swords

ACKNOWLEDGEMENTS AND PRAISE

Hook, Line and Sinker (25 Gates of Hell) was just perfection. If anyone were to utter the words that women can't write extreme gore – Pipe would tear them a new one and display it as art! The narrative was snappy, with enough elements of wit and horror to make it personable. It gave me the chills and flashbacks to old 80's slasher movie vibes. A serial killer with a hook for a hand – winning!

Diabolica Britannica wouldn't have been complete without a werewolf story and boy can Janine Pipe deliver on the monster horror. *Footsteps*…the title doesn't instantly strike fear in the heart of its readers, but it is a sinister undertone in an atmosphere of dread and panic. Another author that can set a scene and it impregnate it in your psyche and it takes root and makes itself at home. The safety of home and a locked door is a faded memory. My eyes grew to the size of saucers and I'm not ashamed to say that I had a few WTF moments. A heavy and intense read that will make monster lovers extremely happy!
Yvonne – The Coy Caterpillar.

"*Should Have Gone to Vegas*" (*The One That Got Away*) – Do you like buddy tales that go wrong? Fan of Adam Nevill's *The Ritual*, perhaps, or unusual creatures? This story was laugh-out-loud funny, wickedly dark, and another reason why I will always read whatever Janine Pipe releases.
Jennifer Soucy

Footsteps by Janine Pipe: Just...wow! Loved this short tale complete with its prologue. I have a fondness for stories that start off going in one direction and then end in a completely different one. Bravo!
Char's Horror Corner

For me personally, the highlight of the second half was '*The Invitation*' (*Graveyard Smash*). The set up was swift, the usage of text messages between daughter and mom was bang-on needed for the story and the ending hits you like a ton of bricks. Great story and I'd love to see more of just what that world is.
Steve Stred

"*The Invitation*" (*Graveyard Smash*) - It's hard to lay out what I liked about this story without spoilers, or at least affecting the reader's experience. I will say that it's well-plotted and Pipe's use of misdirection is Prestige-level. "Are you watching closely?"
Brennan Lefaro

ABOUT THE AUTHOR

Janine has enjoyed horror from early age, frightening herself with ghost stories and learning the craft from King.

After trading in a police badge and an apple for the teach (ing assistant) er, she decided to try her hand at something she loved – writing her own scary stories. She has many terrifying tales published in anthologies which can be found via her Amazon page.

Her story, Footsteps, from the charity anthology Diabolica Britannica, was nominated for a 2020 Splatterpunk Award.

Janine also contributes to Scream Magazine, Cemetery Dance, Horror DNA, Horror Oasis and Night Worms and is a booktuber. As well as writing, she is an editor and publicist for Kandisha Press with her BFF Jill, where she is always on the lookout for new women's voices for their anthologies.

Her current favourite authors and influences are quite obvious when you read this collection. But she'd like to remind you they are – Glenn Rolfe, Hunter Shea and Tim Meyer.

When not writing, reading or reviewing, Janine can be found at home with her husband and daughter, planning their next trip to Walt Disney World and drinking obscene amounts of coffee.

Printed in Great Britain
by Amazon